TWENTY PAGEANTS LATER

TWENTY PAGEANTS LATER

Caroline B. Cooney

BANTAM BOOKS

NEW YORK • TORONTO • LONDON • SYDNEY • AUCKLAND

TWENTY PAGEANTS LATER
A Bantam Book / May 1991

The Starfire logo is a registered trademark of Bantam Books,
a division of Bantam Doubleday Dell Publishing Group, Inc.
Registered in U.S. Patent and Trademark offices and elsewhere.

Copyright © 1991 by Caroline B. Cooney.

Book design by Joseph Rutt.

Library of Congress Cataloging-in-Publication Data

Cooney, Caroline B.
Twenty pageants later / Caroline B. Cooney.
p.   cm.
Summary: As the younger and plainer sister of a frequent beauty
contest winner, fourteen-year-old Scottie-Ann has always had mixed
feelings about such competitions especially when she finds herself a
reluctant contestant in the Marsh Mid Princess Pageant.
ISBN 0-553-07254-4
{1. Beauty contests—Fiction. 2. Self-perception—Fiction.
3. Interpersonal relations—Fiction. 4. Sisters—Fiction.
5. Schools—Fiction. 6. Contests—Fiction.} I. Title.
PZ7.C7834Tw 1991
{Fic}—dc20   90-48248
CIP
AC

Published simultaneously in the United States and Canada

Bantam Books are published by Bantam Books, a division of Bantam Doubleday Dell
Publishing Group, Inc. Its trademark, consisting of the words "Bantam Books" and the
portrayal of a rooster, is Registered in U.S. Patent and Trademark Office and in other
countries. Marca Registrada. Bantam Books, 666 Fifth Avenue, New York, New York
10103.

PRINTED IN THE UNITED STATES OF AMERICA

BVG   0 9 8 7 6 5 4 3 2 1

1

My sister did research and found out that you have a much better chance of being Miss America if you are from Texas and have a double first name.

"You could at least have named me Kristi-Lou," she scolded our parents. "Or Kelly-Marie. But no. You had to call me Dane. It doesn't even look like a girl's name. They'll probably cancel my application because they'll think I'm some guy from Scandinavia."

She was worried about the Miss Teenage America Pageant, which you must enter by mail. It was supposed to be a scholarship program, so first they had to eliminate by grade point average, and once that was out of the way, it could go back to being a beauty contest.

My sister demanded permission to use my name. "Scottie-Anne. Now, there's a name for a beauty pageant. Give me your name," she ordered.

I said it was my name and I was keeping it. "You got the looks and the figure," I pointed out. "I should at least get a decent name."

My sister smiled happily. She knew she had the looks and the figure. Sixteen years old, and the most beautiful girl in the state. She has entered, since age two, some sixty pageants, placed in most, and won nineteen. "Dane McKane," she said reproachfully to our parents. "It rhymes, it matches, it's stupid."

"I'm sorry," said Mother humbly. "I thought it was cute."

"I am too old for cute," said Dane. "Did you think I would be two years old forever? Winning Miss Adorable Preschool pageants for decades?"

I admire Dane when she is a princess onstage, but it is another thing entirely to have a princess in the van with you.

Dane is beautiful. She has fine bones, deep blue eyes, rosy cheeks, an ivory complexion, naturally blond hair with naturally silvery highlights, adorable little seashell ears, a generous, crowd-pleasing smile, and soft, loving lips over perfect white teeth. She has a great figure and has not eaten in several years. She wears bathing suits

2

without straps so that she will tan without marks, but sunshine being hard on the skin, she prefers to stay out of the sun. Her hands are slender and graceful and her fingernails long and sexy. Her feet are narrow and her ankles trim.

Keeping up her body is a full-time occupation. Dane hardly has time for school. Of course, skipping three meals a day frees up lots of time.

We were on our way to the Hyatt Regency for the Miss Coast-to-Coast American Teen Pageant. It's new, commercial, and not yet coast to coast. Eleven states have franchises. "If you win, Dane," I said to her, as a loving sister should, "you'll actually be Miss Somewhere in the Middle of America Teen."

"Shut up, Scottie-Anne," said Dane.

"Don't say that to your sister, Dane," said our father. "Scottie-Anne, don't put Dane down." I've decided that one of my father's most important roles in life is to make each of us apologize to the other.

Dane was nervous. Once backstage, she'd look at the girls she was up against, dismiss three-quarters of them with a superior laugh, and be shaken to her core by the rest. There is never a contest you absolutely *know* you'll win. There is always at least one, or half a dozen, other girls who are as beautiful, as experienced, and as beautifully dressed.

Dane would rather lose altogether than be a runner-up. She says *runner-up* sounds like a slave, somebody who runs up to do errands at your command.

In the van, hurtling down the highway, we were in a portable successwagon, where nobody ever utters the terrible words *second place*. We're *building*. That's how Dane's coach puts it. "Build, Dane!" she cries. "Build!" Dane works so hard and so seriously it does rather resemble bricklaying: getting ready!—readier!—readiest!—for Miss Teenage America.

That is Dane's life goal.

And she does not want it next year. She wants it this year.

In June. When she's still sixteen.

In the olden days, before Dane was a teenager and therefore qualified for Serious Beauty Pageants, we went to pageants in school auditoriums, Elks Clubs, and Veterans of Foreign Wars Halls. I was always in a coma from boredom.

Now we go to fine hotels everywhere: Sheratons, Hyatts, Plazas. I spend every weekend riding in glass elevators, sampling buffets in trellis rooms, and wandering through governors' ballrooms.

Dane was missing dance routine practice for a vital state pageant in order to be in Miss Coast-to-Coast Teen. On the other hand, it would be good practice; she'd pick up a lot of hardware, since she usually also won Miss Congeniality and Miss Photogenic. Plus, if she won, she didn't have to do anything afterward: no Automobile Mall Midnight Madness Sale appearances, or anything. Just take the prizes and run. In this case the prizes were a free modeling course (Dane has already

4

won a dozen free modeling courses), a gift pack of videos, a professional photographer's portfolio, and a flight to Orlando, Florida, which my father would probably sell in the classified ads.

We had to kill the entire day; this was one of those minor pageants where the girls would practice from nine in the morning till four in the afternoon, and the pageant itself would begin at five and last (in my opinion) forevermore.

My father usually finds a bowling alley somewhere in whatever city we're in and spends the entire day bowling. He shows up on time to applaud for Dane in the audience. My mother just waits, in case Dane needs mending, alterations, or rehemming.

Dane has her gowns designed for her by Micharde-Miquelle. Micharde-Miquelle is actually a husband and wife team named Bill and Marcy Williams. They do a lot of pageant gowns in our part of the country, and their gowns are winners. Dane's dresses have many sequins and slits, but not very many sleeves or collars. Depending on her coach's analysis of the pageant, she will wear a virginal peach, white, or rose gown. Judges don't like knock-your-eyes-out scarlet, purple, or royal blue.

I do not know why evening gowns are not made to the standards of Levi's and Wrangler; while blue jeans last for years, evening gowns hardly ever last fifteen minutes. My mother is always in there madly stitching something up or tacking something down.

Coach doesn't come to that many pageants.

Dane's coach is Suzette March. If you're into beauty pageants, you've heard of Suzette March; people come from six states (so she claims) to take advantage of Suzette's coaching. Right now I believe she has seventeen patients. She doesn't call them patients, of course. I am the author of that term. I think they're all mental.

I want to stay home alone instead of attend the pageants.

But Mother and Father say fourteen is too young to stay home alone for a weekend, and although I have loads of friends, there are no mothers willing to adopt me on weekends. So here I was at the Hyatt Regency.

We disembarked from the van. Ours is a custom van, extra long, with hanging space for gowns, mirrors for Dane, a desk in front of my own swivel chair in the way back so I can do homework, and a lockup for the video and camera equipment. Some people don't realize how much it takes to be on the beauty pageant circuit. It takes time *and* money if you want to do it right. Most people think a pretty girl just shows up and struts. It's not that way at all. We carried Dane's necessities into the lobby. The Hyatt Regency was spectacular: acres of marble floors, and stacked reflecting pools over which a white grand piano balanced on a cantilevered stage. We passed the piano, the pools, the green marble, and the black marble. We took escalators up to the balconied second floor, where crystal chandeliers hung just out of reach of children or drunks eager to test their courage.

The registration table had no line, which was miraculous; Mother and Dane went straight up, confirmed payment, and were given all necessary papers and Dane's sash. A rush of girls came just as Dane took her number (eleven). Gauging the competition is routine for me now: They were losers, every one. Except . . . oh, wow! . . . one of them. . . . I stared at her.

Dane stared at her.

The entire hotel seemed to stare at her.

This girl was breathtaking. Dane is lovely, but nobody gasps when they see her. For a moment Dane lost her poise and wet her lips with fear. I hid my fear; I muttered to Dane, "Cows, all of them."

"Do you think so?" She was panicked.

"Absolutely."

"What about that one with the black hair, and the cherry red lips, and the smile—oh, Scottie-Anne, her smile!"

"Hips," I said succinctly.

Dane looked carefully. "It depends on the judges," she said. "Maybe they won't care."

"Then what kind of judges are they?" I demanded.

Dane nodded. "These little commercial contests, though. The judges are probably a bridal shop owner, a woman who modeled twenty years ago for a week, and the substitute noontime television anchor."

We giggled. "Definitely the kind to take off points for hips," I said.

Dane gave me her real smile. She doesn't use it much;

she's resting her lips from all her hours of fake smiles. Her real smile is quiet, shows no teeth, and is, in fact, rather sad. "Love ya, Scots," she said. She disappeared backstage, my mother carrying all of her things, and Dane carrying none.

Eight hours till the pageant, and nothing to do. I have developed more patience than any fourteen-year-old in the twentieth century.

Right now I need all the patience I can get. My best friend, Lillie, until last week sane, has decided she, too, wants to get into beauty pageants.

We go to Marshfield Middle School. This is a blessing, because eighth grade is safely removed from Dane, who is in eleventh at the high school. I am not excited about next year, when I'll be in the same building as Dane and teachers will shriek, "Dane McKane is *your sister?* Oh, my goodness! I never would have suspected!"

Marsh Mid is going to raise money to buy new encyclopedias by having a beauty pageant. Now, I personally feel that anybody who participates in a beauty pageant will never *use* an encyclopedia, wouldn't recognize an encyclopedia if you lined the refrigerator shelves with one, but I'm not on student council and I didn't come up with a better idea, so beauty pageant it is.

Marsh Mid Princess.

Catchy, huh? Has that swampy ring.

Lillie plans to enter. Saturday she spent the night at our house, leafing through Dane's photo albums (practically a lifetime undertaking, there are so many) and asking Dane for advice. Dane loves it when younger girls are adoring. She shimmers for them, as if they themselves were lights, camera, and action. Sometimes I think Dane is never off the runway; she has moved permanently into Display Mode.

Dane's advice was for naught because, Lillie came sadly back to report, her parents refused to give permission to enter.

"But why is that?" cried my parents, upset for poor Lillie.

"Beauty pageants are sick and depraved," Lillie explained, with a certain lack of tact.

"I beg your pardon!" My mother was beside herself. My mother, in her words, "came from nothing." If I were Grandma and Grandpa, I would not let that go by without an argument. My mother lied about her age so she could work after school in a high-paying job; she quit high school at sixteen and later on went back nights for her General Equivalency Diploma. She has always taken the job that offers the most benefits. *Benefits* means, will it pay doctors' bills? She has never held a job she likes. I've always wondered why she couldn't find a job she liked and still get good benefits, but I've never discussed this with her. When Dane was two years old, Mother entered her in a Tiny Tot Modeling Pageant, and Mother had so much fun, they never stopped. She loves a pageant; it never loses its Cinderella appeal for her. Mother never gets bored.

"My mom," explained Lillie, "says they're meat markets."

Meat would have frozen under our mother's glare.

Dane just laughed. "I've heard that line before, Lillie. You *are* meat. We're all meat. Under the skin, we're all hamburger."

Lillie pondered that. "I think she meant nice girls don't parade their bodies for men."

Dane really laughed this time. "There are no men at beauty pageants. Just little brothers and fathers. Believe me, I've been trying to meet guys at these things for years."

Then my sister did something I had never seen her do. Leaning forward, looking intensely into Lillie's eyes, Dane said, "Put pressure on your parents, Lillie. Make them sign the permissions for the beauty pageant. You," said my sister softly, "have *potential*."

Lillie repeated that at least a thousand times during the following days. "But Mom! Dane says I have potential. And Dane has won all kinds of beauty contests. She's been everything from Miss Greater Waterbury to Miss All–New England. From Miss Valentine's Day to Miss Perfect Teen."

Lillie's mother was unmoved. I love that about Lillie's parents. They listen to every argument and every argument achieves nothing. Whereas my parents come unglued and waffle around, and if we push, we win.

Lillie said, "Do you think my boobs are good enough?"

10

Lillie's mother screamed a neighborhood-waking, squad-car-summoning scream, as of one being raped and knifed. "I can't stand it! Don't call them boobs. I hate that word. You may never, never, never, never, never, never enter a bathing suit contest. I will shoot you first. Somebody go buy a gun."

"I hate when you threaten homicide, Beverly," said Lillie's father.

"Would you rather I threatened suicide? It's her or me."

"There aren't bathing suits," said Lillie. "It's just a middle school pageant. There will be talent and then party dress. Dane says I can borrow one of her gowns."

"I feel sick," said Lillie's mother. "I feel like moving back to Dallas. Does anybody remember why we moved here next door to the McKanes, anyway?"

"Dallas would be great!" said Lillie eagerly. "Dane says all the national beauty pageant winners are from Texas. So if we move back to Texas—"

"We'll move to a ranch so remote we won't even get television reception, let alone be able to tune in the Miss America Pageant," said Lillie's mother. "Scottie-Anne, tell her it's out of the question. Tell her beauty pageants are sick and demented and everybody in them is mental."

Mrs. Gold was quoting me. But I couldn't agree this time, or Lillie would abandon me. Then I'd have to be best friends with Lillie's mother instead. Great. Eighth grade and my best friend would be forty.

Lillie said to her mother, "I have more talent than Dane, anyway."

In deference to the fact that I was listening, Mrs. Gold deleted her opinion of Dane's talents.

About half your beauty pageants do not require a talent, other than walking down the runway, which, believe me, is about nine hundred times harder than it looks. But the other half—well, that's when Dane's difficulty arises. Dane basically has no talents. We have been fighting this problem for years.

Talent, regrettably, is limited to what can be demonstrated onstage.

Spelling, for example, does not count as a talent, which is too bad, because Dane has never misspelled a word in her life; in fact, she's taking both Spanish and French now and has never misspelled anything in either of those languages, either. But you can't saunter onstage and pass the judges your spelling quizzes. Dane enjoyed horseback riding and even won some ribbons, but you cannot take a horse onstage with you. She's pretty decent in tennis, too, but there again, they won't let you put up a net and whack a few balls. As for her final, unbeatable talent, nobody yet has won the talent categories on the strength of being able to beat the neighborhood at video games.

Music and dance are the preferred talents. So far we have had to accept failure with singing, flute, and violin. And let me tell you, Dane does not easily accept failure. There were many long, excruciating hours, adding up to painful years, in which I (the listener) suffered even more than Dane (the practicer). There was no option but to stay with dance. She has studied ballet, jazz, ballroom, and modern. At best, Dane is fair.

With grim determination, Dane decided on tap for her talent because audiences love it. She practices twice a day, no matter what. The rest of us could be in bed with the flu, staggering around having chicken soup and aspirin, and Dane would be tap dancing.

Lillie said, "I did, after all, win the symphony's Young Musician Competition. I will be onstage with the orchestra."

Instruments are tricky talents. Trombone, say—out of the question. Play a brass instrument, and your cheeks puff out; you wouldn't be beautiful; you'd lose points. Drums—not romantic. Beauty queens can't whap away at two tympani and some snare drums. Stringed instruments, like violins, are always good—unless they're guitars; guitars lack romance, too. However, now and then somebody plays a banjo or a ukulele and gets away with it.

But piano is perfect. What could be more graceful than a beautiful girl, a long gown, a grand piano, and Chopin?

Lillie's parents paid as much for her grand piano as my parents paid for the van in which we haul Dane from state to state.

I looked at Lillie again and thought, Dane's right.

Lillie has potential. Furthermore, her boobs are fine. I've judged billions. I should know.

But, of course, I didn't say so. Mrs. Gold would have killed me, and I was looking forward to school the next week. I love school. Eighth grade has the best teachers and the best boys, every one of whom this year suddenly turned into a person. I actually like them. I actually daydream about the boys in class now instead of rock stars. I didn't make cheerleading, didn't make field hockey, and none of my art got into the winter exhibit. But somehow eighth grade is so much fun.

Normally you don't judge your best friend; she's who she is, and that's that. I found myself judging Lillie for points. She's unusual, and that's not good. Judges don't like unusual. She's exotic: half Yugoslav, or Serbo-Croatian, or something mountainous. It gives her this dark Egyptian princess look. Judges lean toward blond Princess Diana looks . . . Dane McKane looks. But Lillie has presence: that wonderful command of body and audience which most girls can train for a lifetime to acquire and not get.

Mrs. Gold said, "Lillie. You were named for your grandmother. Who would be very proud of you and your academic success and exceptionally proud that, at only fourteen, you have already begun what we are sure will be a brilliant musical career. Let's not tarnish that with some silly, stupid, degrading beauty pageant."

Of course, I had said that myself a thousand times, but it is one thing for *me* to betray my sister. It is another thing to sit there while other people do it. "Mrs. Gold, I happen to be very proud of Dane and her success."

The Golds were stopped dead by the size of that lie.

"I think Lillie should enter the Marsh Mid Pageant," I said, "because she will gain poise, self-confidence, and stage ability."

"Wow," said Lillie. "If some angel in the sky is keeping track, will you ever get sisterly points for that."

Mrs. Gold leaned way down over me, her long, thin nose almost touching mine. Her glasses slid forward, as if to switch noses. She pursed her face into a drawstring bag of lips. "Scottie-Anne McKane," she said, "Lillie has my permission to enter the Marsh Mid Princess Pageant . . . on one condition."

"What's that?"

"You have to enter, too."

2

※

So here we were at the Hyatt, waiting to see if my lovely sister could whip that black-haired beauty.

I tried to imagine saying to Dane, "Oh, by the way, I've decided to enter a beauty pageant myself. Want to help?"

Would Dane choke laughing, saying things like, "God himself couldn't give anybody that much help." Or would she say kindly, "Why, Scottie-Anne, what a sweet idea. You do have a hyphenated name. Maybe that will make up for—well—the other aspects."

16

Father appeared, in a bad mood because they weren't going to let parents take their own videos; you had to buy the pageant's video, at seventy-five bucks a film. These commercial pageants get you in every way; you have to pay a stiff registration fee, buy advertising in the program, supply professional photographs of the contestant . . . it adds up when, like Dane, you do this all year long.

The Navy installation had sent its band. Pageants are very patriotic. They always remind me of Little League: how at the first game, the high school band plays and you sing the "Star-Spangled Banner" and salute the flag and get all teary.

Blaring fanfares rocked the auditorium. The band director, uniform covered with gold braid and glittering medallions, launched into "God Bless America." The colors were presented. The audience stood.

My father had his Polaroid. He'd get his own shots of Dane when she was coming down the runway and— he hoped—accepting the crown.

The master of ceremonies, black tuxedo, scarlet bow tie, and cummerbund, walked forward carrying his mike and spoke over the band anthem, his voice rich, like hot chocolate. "Ladies and gentlemen . . ."

I had my program. Five more dollars. My judging technique is easy: I bring a thick Magic Marker and draw big X's through the photographs of the girls I'm eliminating. Mother keeps a three-ring notebook with special charts she designed for ease in grading.

Backstage, Dane would be harsh with tension, the real Dane gone, replaced by a Barbie doll of perfection. I think she is a little frightening, and it always amazes me that, time after time, she gets Miss Congeniality. There wouldn't be one of those today; the girls hadn't been here long enough to recognize each other across the stage, let alone vote.

". . . the current Miss Coast-to-Coast Teen . . . Laurette Benoir!" shouted the emcee.

The audience burst into applause.

Dane is addicted to applause. The sound of it makes her breathe faster, brings a sparkle to her eyes.

She was back there in a line, ready for display, taking the arm of her assigned escort, and soaking up the applause—praying that by the end of the night all applause would be hers.

Every other girl was praying the same thing. We read when we studied World War I that "there are no atheists in a foxhole." Well, there are no atheists at beauty pageants, either.

One by one, forty-three girls were presented. Each state had sent its runners-up, too; it was going to be a long evening.

We had terrific seats because my mother had claimed them at about nine in the morning and spread our coats all over them. Seating is almost always first come, first choose; we are always first come. I have spent my life on folding chairs in the front row opposite judges and next to a runway.

18

The first five girls were somewhat pretty. Maximum compliment. My heart ached for them. Did they really believe they were stunning? Did they really think that the right mascara and the right blush turned them into beauty queens? Were their mothers and fathers actually convinced that their little girl was the most beautiful girl "coast to coast"?

Number Six was so plain I had to look down. It was embarrassing.

If I enter Marsh Mid, I thought, people will be embarrassed for me. *Look at the poor little McKane girl trying to be a beauty queen like her sister. You'd think the parents would say no just to save her the humiliation.*

Poor Number Six wore heels so high she couldn't balance. She tottered to the center of the stage, so afraid of audience and judges that, instead of smiling, she bared her teeth at the ceiling like an orangutan. It's very hard to look into the eyes of the judges; only the best contestants pull it off. She didn't know what to do with her escort, either. When it was time to pirouette in the middle of the runway, showing off all sides of herself, she just left him there and walked around him, as if he were a post. Warrior style, he stood motionless, expressionless, and obedient.

She tried a sexy pose, putting one hand on her hip and making the hip jut out, but she lost her balance and had to stick the other foot out to catch herself. There she stood, legs spread as if mounting a horse.

Pageant audiences are kind to losers. Like Little

League again: All the parents give you points for trying. At a ball game, if you didn't swing at a pitch, the parents yell comfortingly, "Good eye, good eye!" Poor, tortured Number Six had survived without collapse. She received so much applause that it perked her up into a totally irrational belief she was going to win, after all.

Number Seven was much better looking, although somewhat hard. You never wear really brilliant red lipstick or really bright blue eye shadow because it has a hardening effect and judges like soft.

Number Eight was thin as a pencil. No figure whatsoever. She could model, but she was no beauty queen. Judges like curves.

I occupied myself drawing large X's.

". . . number eleven!" shouted the emcee into the mike. They always yell. Everything they say is important to somebody. "Miss Dane McKane!"

We clapped madly. If the contest had been closer to home, we'd have brought friends, but we'd left at five in the morning, plus the wait, and even my grandparents aren't in the running for that.

"Dane is sixteen years old," shouted the emcee. "Blond! And five foot six!" I'm told in the olden days the emcee also shouted out every girl's measurements. Emcees like to make suggestive remarks, but they don't actually say "thirty-five, twenty-four, thirty-seven" anymore.

Dane's escort was huge. Clearly a former football player, now a junior lieutenant, he took up so much space I wondered if they'd both fit on the runway. When Dane smiled at the audience, she stretched out a hand as if to take their applause in her palm, and they gave it to her. Twice what the first ten girls had heard.

They were acknowledging beauty.

People all around muttered, "She's competition!" "Lord, look at that smile!" "Been in lots of contests, that one."

My mother glowed. Father was much too busy taking photographs to hear.

Dane has such stage presence. Halfway down, she stopped her escort, thanked him prettily, and walked to the end of the runway alone. None of the previous ten had done that.

"Dane is a junior at Marshfield High School in Connecticut," said the emcee. Dane swayed from the hips. The slit gown revealed her thigh at just the right angle: more model's display than openly sexual. The audience loved it and clapped again.

"Dane tap dances," said the emcee. "She's a member of the student council, an honor roll student, a soup kitchen volunteer at her church, and in her spare time—" he laughed; the audience laughed; you're much more of a winner if it's clear you have no spare time; have never had spare time; you're much too busy helping your community and being a success—"Dane likes to play video games and ride horses."

Dane smiled generously at the audience, as if letting

them in on secrets. The only secret was she hadn't been on a horse in two years. As for the soup kitchen, Dane's turn comes up one Saturday a month, and so far she's had practices every Saturday and Mother's done it for her.

"Dane McKane," repeated the emcee, savoring the rhyme. "Number eleven! Thank you, Dane!"

Dane bowed gently to the audience, thanked her escort again, and blew a soft kiss to the emcee, who caught it in his hand and smiled at her.

Points, points, points.

At the Marsh Mid Princess Pageant, we will charge five dollars for admission. Everybody will come. The programs will be donated by the newspaper, girls' photographs by the Snap Shoppe. High school students taking appropriate classes will run the lights, take the videos, provide music, and so forth. We expect to net a thousand dollars. It is amazing how much encyclopedias cost.

The girl with the black hair was number thirty-eight. When he introduced her, the emcee (relaxing more than he ought to) yelled, "Number thirty-eight, ladies and gentlemen! Morgana-Lisa Maxson. And is she ever a thirty-eight! Wow!"

You never wear a dress that overpowers you; the focus has to be on you, not the fabric or the cut. This dress was a knockout diagonally cut in three sections: Glittering black, pulsing midnight blue, and sequined royal blue clung to her body. She definitely wore no underwear. She was not only a thirty-eight, she was magnificent.

While Dane's hair was tucked sweetly back by invisible combs, curled southern Civil War belle style, Thirty-eight's thick, black hair was loose, cascading over bare, white-as-snow shoulders. It swirled as she did, a cape of sensuality she carried as easily as a glove. It's difficult for beginners to wear a strapless gown; it can slither out of place during the maneuvers you're required to make. Strapless presented no difficulty for Thirty-eight. When she turned—slowly, sexily—the gown had no back. She was bare almost to the base of her spine.

The audience went wild clapping.

My parents, stiff with worry, clapped courteously. This was a winner. Had we come all this way—to a pageant meant to be merely a building block; a nothing regional commercial pageant—to lose to Morgana-Lisa Maxson?

And what a name! Morgana-Lisa Maxson, my foot. Probably born Debbie Jones.

The pageant went on and on, as pageants do.

We had breaks now and then. Father sent me to get Cokes from the vending machine. "Get a Diet Pepsi for your sister," he ordered me, "and take it backstage."

There was no Diet anything; when I went backstage and told Dane she had to partake of calories, she nearly swatted me. "I'll have water," she said, furious.

She was afraid.

23

Morgana-Lisa Maxson stood alone in the center of the room, as if she already ruled, and had chosen Empty Space to be her escort. The remaining contestants huddled in groups, or leaned against walls.

I have never met anybody who hates losing as much as my sister. To Dane, losing is practically criminal. She isn't a sore loser; she doesn't kick the winner. For weeks she takes it out on herself, attacking life and practice with such grim determination you'd think she planned to grind herself into shape.

Morgana-Lisa Maxson looked our way and smiled. A victorious, simpering, *I'm better than you are—nyah, nyay-nyah-nyah, nyah!* smile.

I saw us as Morgana-Lisa must. A beautiful, gentle, slender blonde (outclassed) with her dumpy little sister running errands. "Whip her ass, Dane," I said.

Dane giggled. Her whole body loosened up. "Why, Scottie-Anne McKane, have you joined my team? What did I do to rate this?" She sauntered toward the water fountain and simpered back at Morgana-Lisa Maxson. Thirty-eight grinned even wider, not scared a bit.

I went back to the auditorium.

"How's she doing?" whispered Father.

"Nervous."

"Me, too," said Father. "Thirty-eight's bad."

Nobody talked about what it would be like living with Dane if she lost a two-bit regional like this. She had told everybody at the state contest that she was getting in "a little practice." They expected her to sashay back laden with hardware. If she came back without a single medal . . .

Semifinals.

From the forty-three, they chose eight.

I wasn't too nervous for semifinals. Dane had to be one of the eight, and, of course, she was. But she was chosen last, and it was tense. For the group picture, she had to stand next to Morgana-Lisa Maxson. The contrast was startling. Dane—so sweet, so fragile. Morgana-Lisa—voluptuous, stunning, demanding.

My mother shrugged. "It's whatever the judges like," she said. "If they go for that overdone, mature, centerfold look, we're finished."

I didn't think the boys in high school would consider Morgana-Lisa overdone or mature. But they'd definitely put her picture on their locker doors. In the same dress.

Each of the eight paraded again.

Of course, most of the audience was out of the picture: relatives and friends of the now discarded thirty-five. But since those girls had to stay onstage for a group song, nobody could leave. If you let the losers depart as they lose, you'd also lose your audience, your applause, and your video sales.

The eight were desperately hiding their desperation.

I imagined entering a beauty pageant myself. My hands went damp. No way! I would never put myself through that!

Then came "interviews." Each girl was asked a question, written by the judges, and read to her by the emcee.

Thirty-eight was asked, "Morgana-Lisa, do you think the changing situation in Europe is going to be a good thing for America?"

They love questions about what's happening in the world. I hoped that Morgana-Lisa didn't know what was changing in Europe. Or even what Europe was.

Nope. In a mellifluous voice Morgana-Lisa said, "I am very excited that new freedom is being earned by millions of innocent people formerly under Communist rule! The innovation, the effort, the imagination and commitment that is being exhibited, can only help America, which is, of course, the heart of innovation and commitment itself!"

Applause, applause, applause.

You just couldn't answer anything better.

My mother broke her grading pencil in half, she was so tense.

We were sick when it was Dane's turn. Dane can never remember geography. She says everything in Central America is alike, all squashed in the curve and growing marijuana; she says Eastern Europe is all alike, everybody working in factories and standing in breadlines.

I knotted my hands.

"Dane," said the emcee, "homelessness is a big problem in our country right now. What would you do about it, if you had power?"

26

Wonderful. Dane would probably say, *Well, there are lots of houses for sale in our town. Let those homeless people buy a ranch house.*

My father swore under his breath. He's always coaching Dane on important issues, and Dane never quite gets it.

My sister said, "America is a wonderful country, and if some of our children don't have proper homes, it's a sad and terrible thing. I would get real close to the problem, and talk to some of the innocent victims, and discuss it with our senators and representatives. In my work at the soup kitchen, I see some of this and my heart goes out to people caught in such unfortunate circumstances."

The audience went wild. People in the back even whistled. You can't go wrong when you throw America and innocence into your answer.

"Thank you, Dane," said the emcee.

"Thank you, God," said my father.

We three giggled under our breath.

Then came the awful time when the judges confer.

I don't know what they've been doing all evening long, but now they do it some more. They conferred, and judged, and conferred.

The naval band played a selection of John Philip Sousa marches. Nobody was in a march mood. We just wanted to know whether Dane or Morgana-Lisa was going to be Miss Coast-to-Coast Teen, and whether the

27

one that was first runner-up would behave herself or deliver a well-placed backstage kick.

Finally the judges were ready.

Last year's Miss Coast-to-Coast Teen reappeared, gleaming, glittering, and fully crowned.

The emcee took his envelope. Read its contents. Shook his head. Beamed at his audience. Kept the suspense going.

"And the third runner-up!" he bellowed. "Miss Jennie Marraco!"

Jennie struggled to look happy about being fourth. She jumped up and down a little.

"And the second runner-up!" he yelled. "Miss Nicole Jeanne Curtis!"

The second runner-up at least had somebody to hug. Nicole Jeanne and Jennie linked arms at the waist and beamed at each other.

Dane was still smiling. She has unbelievable smile control. She can smile for hours. I smile for sixty seconds and my face hurts.

I knew that even if she was runner-up and not Miss Coast-to-Coast Teen, she would smile on and on, like a turnpike without end.

The emcee strung it out. "Ladies . . ." he purred into his mike, turning to smile at one side of the audience. ". . . and gentlemen . . ." he turned to the other side. The pageant's cameraman swiveled his camera. "I am so proud of our first runner-up! What a good job the judges did! Ladies . . . and gentlemen . . .

28

parents . . . sisters . . . brothers . . . grandparents . . . our first runner-up . . . is . . .

". . . Morgana-Lisa Maxson!"

Dane's smile went real. She flung her head back, momentarily escaping the audience, and then came back, trembling with relief. She hugged the losers without bothering to look at them, even at Morgana-Lisa Maxson, because as of that moment, Thirty-eight had ceased to matter to anybody.

Father was on his feet whistling and stomping. Mother was biting her lips to hold in her delight. Father—who would never weep—loves to show joy. Mother—who dislikes showing joy—loves to weep.

Regally, Dane approached last year's queen.

The crown was fragile, like my sister.

The former queen had trouble fitting it on Dane's hair. Dane whispered something which made the queen pull back in a hurry. *Mess my hair and die,* was probably the gist of it. In the Starlight Princess Northeast Pageant one of the competition had sabotaged Dane—spilling makeup on her gown and pretending it was an accident. "Let me fix your hair!" the girl had cried. "Only if you want a Coke bottle down your throat," Dane had replied, advancing. The backstage manager had had to separate them.

I was eager to get out of there, but we had to sit while Dane walked alone down the runway in her new crown, the band played, the sponsors got named, the prizes were given out, and so forth and so on.

Then Mother went backstage to help with photographs and packing. It would take hours. I leaned against the wall in the hall outside the dressing rooms and listened to parents talk.

"I didn't want that blond girl to get it. I am so sick of skinny and blond winning all the time."

"That black-haired one was a little too obvious."

"Still. That blonde had won a lot of pageants. She was a professional. You could tell she'd had training and everything. I don't think it's fair when girls like that can be in pageants with my daughter, who's absolutely beautiful but hasn't had the experience."

Nobody at a pageant admires the winner.

They want their daughter/sister/girlfriend to be the winner.

The losers emerged fairly quickly.

"Darling, you were so beautiful!" cried their families. "We were so proud of you up there!"

Each girl tried to look proud and beautiful. Chins quivered and lips trembled. How sad the elaborate gowns were now, crumpled in plastic bags. How pointless the cases of makeup and hot rollers.

"I had a good time," they all said, with false, desperate conviction. "It was worth it. I'm glad I did it," they all said.

Marsh Mid Princess, I said to myself, is a little junior high nothing. A fund-raiser. I believe in encyclopedias. I can enter, Lillie can enter, we'll have fun, it'll be worth it. I don't have to win. I'll be glad I tried.

In the van going home, as my parents admired the Polaroids of Dane, I sat in the back, pretending to listen to my Walkman.

I listened to my heart.

Don't get near it! Don't hope. Don't yearn. You can't win anything, let alone a beauty pageant.

But I was no different from the rest.

I hoped.

3

Monday mornings and Friday afternoons at school, we have short assemblies. We get lectures on what is coming up, how poorly we behaved last time, how we aren't going to be like that again, are we? and little films on drunk driving, AIDS, the dangers of strangers, and how not to get pregnant. Usually they skimp on details that could be important and instead give us philosophy, or what we dismiss as preachy talk.

In Monday's assembly, application forms for the Marshfield Middle School Princess Pageant were passed out.

The teacher/sponsor was Mrs. Craven, a fine woman about sixty years old, who weighs perhaps two hundred pounds. Mrs. Craven announced that she was especially excited about being teacher/adviser for this because, when she was a girl, she had been Miss Georgia.

There was a reverent pause in which we tried to imagine her (a) young, (b) beautiful, and (c) thin.

Nobody could. The girls covered their faces with bent elbows, smothering giggles.

Mrs. Craven said, "Every girl has the capacity to be beautiful. Inner light shines in all of us."

"Must have shined megawatts for you to win," muttered Eric.

We put hands over our mouths to choke back cruel laughter.

"Our training for the Princess Pageant," said Mrs. Craven, beaming, "will include learning how to apply makeup, how to dress, how to walk, and how to smile."

"I mastered walking and smiling by age two," said Eric. "What's the matter with girls? They need Remedial Walking?"

"Skills for our century," intoned Nicholas. "How to stand, turn, and pivot."

"It's the pivoting that's tough," agreed Eric. "That old pivot gets 'em every time."

The boys laughed insanely. Naturally, none of the girls wanted to be caught taking an application form now.

Lillie said sharply, "Shut up, you geeks. I'm beautiful, and I'm going to prove it, so there." She took two applications.

Nicholas said, "What's the matter, Lillie? You figure they won't notice you the first time? You need two tries?"

"It's because she hasn't had Remedial Walking yet," explained Eric.

Nicholas nodded. "Probably needs *pre*–Remedial Walking."

The principal was now standing next to our seats, glaring down. "Nicholas, you are tired of being on the soccer team, I suppose? Eric, you would rather spend your afternoons in my office than at practice?"

"No, sir."

"Sorry, Mr. Shippee."

"We won't laugh at beauty pageants again. Promise," said Nicholas, and immediately both boys exploded into laughter. Nicholas laughed so hard he bounced forward and whacked his forehead against the seat in front of him. "Ow-ey, ow-ey, ow-ey," he moaned dramatically.

I had the weirdest, sickest thought. I wanted to kiss his forehead to make it all better.

The principal put a hand over his own mouth to keep from laughing along. I put a hand over *my* mouth to keep my lips from kissing. "It's a fund-raiser," said Mr. Shippee sternly, "and I expect you gentlemen to assist."

"Gentlemen?" repeated Lillie. "In the eighth grade?"

"Scottie-Anne," said Mr. Shippee, "your sister Dane

has agreed to come to practices and give pointers. Isn't that wonderful?"

What was I supposed to say? *I hate having my sister trespass on my school? I hate having a sister who can show how to be beautiful when all I can show is how to be medium?* I said out loud, "She'll have a great time."

Lillie put an application in my hand.

"Scots!" cried Nicholas. "You aren't really going to do that, are you?"

"Why?" said Lillie fiercely. "You think she can't win?"

"Why would she want to?" protested Nicholas.

"She has to. If Scottie-Anne doesn't enter, I can't enter. My mother said so."

"Your mother's weird," observed Nicholas. "What does Scots have to do with anything?"

"Mrs. Gold figures I'll never agree to it," I explained to Nicholas. "And that way, Lillie can't be in it, either, and the woman in Lillie won't be twisted or degraded. But Lillie thinks she'll win, and she's dying to be in it, and so if we're going to stay friends, I have to be in it, too."

Assembly ended. We were all getting up. People on the inside of the rows were pushing us to get past. Nicholas said, "Lillie, what kind of friend are you?"

An excellent question, and one I had been meaning to ask.

"A winner," said Lillie. She tossed her head in a remarkable, almost perfect copy of Dane's hair-flinging exercises, and departed, spine much straighter than it had been entering the auditorium.

In junior high, you slump. I don't know why. Junior high girls slouch around. You see it in pageants; they beat it out of you in training. It's high school before you're willing to stand tall and aggressive. Lillie had high school posture: runway posture.

Nicholas stared after her. People jostled him. He stepped back inside an empty row while sixth, seventh, and eighth graders shoved to the exit.

Boys and girls have separate gyms. That day, of all days, the gym teacher had to be absent, and the sub had to be a woman who wasn't qualified to sub gym, so we just sat on the polished maple floor and talked. Every girl had her Marsh Mid Princess application. There was a lot of kidding and silliness. Several girls pranced down invisible runways, batting their eyes at judges and flinging their hips at an imaginary audience packed with boys. But we were serious. There wasn't a girl there who didn't read every question on the form and answer it in her heart.

"Weight," read Tasha. "Let's see. I'm five two and weigh ninety-six. I'm a size three, of course."

This shut up everybody who was a twelve, for sure.

But it didn't shut up Shannon. "Miss America is often short, but never skinny, Tasha. I am five foot five, a hundred and ten, and in a bathing suit—"

"There's no bathing suit division," snapped Lillie.

36

"There should be," said Shannon. "I have the best bathing suit."

"You slime," yelled Tasha. "Just because your mother lets you wear a string bikini doesn't mean—"

I said, "How about community activities? Do any of us do anything for the community?"

"I help in the Sunday school nursery," said Jodie.

Apparently nobody else had ever helped anybody. It was sobering. Thirty girls, and only one had contributed to her community. We listed what we could do (basketball, guitar lessons, ice skating, piano), but you could hardly pretend that being goalie on the field hockey team was an act of public generosity.

"We must start an activity," said Lillie firmly. "Everybody think. What could we do to make this a better town?"

"We could get the hottest group to come and give a free rock concert," said Shannon.

"You're right, Tasha," said Lillie. "Shannon is a slime."

After school, of course, Dane was not home: She was at her state pageant rehearsal. Or maybe it was her tap dancing lesson. Or possibly she was having a fitting.

I went over to the Golds'.

Mrs. Gold is the supervisor of town planning, but I guess we don't have that much planning to do, because she only works from nine till one.

"I trust," said Mrs. Gold, "that this whole silly pageant idea has been discarded."

How she could trust that when Lillie had just invested her entire savings in makeup, I did not know.

"Moth-er," said Lillie irritably.

"I don't like how you split those syllables," said Mrs. Gold.

"As soon as Dane is home, I'm trying on her gowns," said Lillie.

"She's away?" said Mrs. Gold hopefully. "On a student abroad program for the winter, perhaps?"

"Moth-er. What's wrong with beauty pageants, anyway?"

"They are shallow."

"What's shallow about being a winner? You wanted me to win the piano competition, didn't you?"

"That's different. You worked for that. A beauty pageant is nothing except what you were born with."

"I was born with your genes, Mother. And Daddy's genes. Aren't you proud of what you produced?"

"Of course I'm proud of you. You're the light of my life."

"Do you think I'm ugly?"

"I think you're beautiful."

"But you don't want anybody else to think so?"

"I want you to be a trial lawyer and back people into corners like this," said Mrs. Gold. "Scottie-Anne, what does Dane expect to get from all her beauty pageants? Other than sashes and trophies, of course?"

What did Dane expect?

Oh, not much. Admirers. Fame. Producers begging her to star in their films. Magazines begging her to be on their covers. Parades begging her to honor them on a float, perhaps with the President.

"I guess she just likes being up in front of people," I said.

"Telephone home, Scottie-Anne," Lillie demanded, "and see if Dane's home yet. When's her next pageant, anyway? I need to watch. And get me her best videos. I have to study her moves."

"Lillie!" cried her mother. "You don't even sound like you! You sound almost fierce!"

"A trial lawyer would be a weakling, maybe?" asked Lillie. "I doubt if Miss America is a weakling, either."

Mrs. Gold was truly upset. She tried to laugh. "This is like a local election," she said. "A person wins a seat on the school board, and all through the politicking, she's fantasizing about being elected President of the United States. First it's Marsh Mid Princess, Lillie, and then it's Miss America."

Lillie did not laugh, which was a clue.

If you laugh, you don't think you'll win. People who laugh have already surrendered, are joining in the joke early, so they aren't laughed at later, when they lose.

Winners never laugh.

"Not Miss America, Mom," said Lillie. "I'm too young. Miss Teenage America, of course."

4

Tuesday the pressure began. "Scots, if you don't get your parents' signature on the form, I can't, either. And we have to submit them Friday."

"I can't enter a pageant, Lillie."

"Of course you can. And anyway, it's a beginner thing. Dane said so herself. A good place to start building."

"I don't have anything to build with, Lillie. Or to. I'm not beautiful."

"You're very nice looking," said Lillie.

40

"You sound like a scout leader," I said glumly. "*Nice* is a word you reach for when nothing more interesting fits. I can't make a fool of myself."

"Scots, we need contestants in order to sell tickets and make gobs of money. What kind of contest will it be if nobody enters?"

"Plenty of girls will enter. Tasha. Shannon. You."

"I can't if you don't!"

"Your parents won't stick to that, Lillie."

"Yes, they will! You don't know them! And even if you're right, Scottie-Anne, I need you. I don't want to do it alone. It's too scary. Shannon and Tasha will be horrible. They're always horrible, but backstage at a beauty pageant they'll be intensely horrible. Please? For me? Because we're best friends?"

Which meant I had to ask my mother and father. At supper, which is the only place I see them. With Dane sitting there.

The Golds don't mind having separate meals. If Mr. Gold has his evening exercise/swim class, and Mrs. Gold has a town planning meeting, and Lillie has a piano lesson, they fix their own suppers separately and eat whatever, whenever.

My mother won't allow it. We eat together if it kills us, and tonight I thought it would.

Dane, of course, was having three kernels of corn, half a biscuit without butter, a piece of white chicken without the skin, a glass of skim milk, and low-cal Jell-O.

"You eat like a hospital patient," I complained. I had noodles with cheese sauce, chicken with skin, and biscuits with honey as well as butter.

"I eat as if I have to fit into my gown next week as well as this week," said Dane.

"How was school today, dear?" my mother asked me.

"Good," I said.

"Details?" she said.

"Nothing happened, Mom. It was just a good day." With lapses.

"My day was excellent, Mother," said Dane. "However, my left ankle seems a little weak. I'm thinking we should see the sports doctor."

"Since when are beauty contests a sport?" I said.

"Tap dancing," said Dane furiously, "is a sport."

"Not an art? Not a skill? Probably not the way you dance, huh?"

"Girls," said Father. He flourished advertising fliers from the newspaper: Radio Shack, Sears, and Bloomingdale's. "Look at these videocams. I no sooner invest in the newest thing than it's superseded by better technology. I cannot believe how lightweight the new ones are. Grace, we've got to get one of these."

"How much are they?"

"Starting at twelve hundred. Up to eighteen hundred."

42

"Jase, we still have a year of payments on the old one."

"Maybe we could sell it."

"We'd take such a beating," said my mother. "Anyway, I'm pretty satisfied with the videotaping we're getting now. Aren't you, Dane?"

"It could be sharper," said Dane. "Sometimes, when the lighting is casting shadows, it would be nice to have a camcorder that automatically compensated. I forgot to tell you. Mr. Shippee asked me to pitch in and help with the Marsh Mid Princess Pageant. Of course, I said I'd be glad to. And, of course, it'll look good on my own applications, that I'm helping younger girls to follow in my footsteps." Dane smiled at her three kernels of corn as if they were appreciative judges. Then she made a face at Mother. "Which might compensate for the name Dane McKane. Did you notice how the emcee last weekend was amused by it? Kept repeating it like a little joke? I still say I should be the one called Scottie-Anne."

I'm named for Mother's parents: Grandpa is Scottie and Grandma is Anne. "You could take your names from the other grandparents," I suggested. "Just think. You could be Chuckie-Dawn."

Dane giggled. "A sobering thought. Who's going to be in the contest, anyway, Scottie-Anne?"

I shrugged with my eyebrows and shoulders, as if the subject hardly mattered. "We haven't passed back applications yet." *Let them say it!* I prayed. *You're eligi-*

ble! You be in it, Scottie-Anne! You have potential! I can't wait to see you!

Mother said, "Who's the adviser?"

"Mrs. Craven."

"Lardbucket?" shrieked Dane. "That's so pitiful."

"She was Miss Georgia when she was young."

"No!" whispered Dane. "Truly? That is so sad. How can she look in her mirror in the morning?"

"The same way I do," I said.

The table was silent.

"But Scottie-Anne, darling," said my mother at last, "you have very *nice* features."

Wednesday, Dane and I had supper at the Golds'. We do not routinely do this. No doubt Mr. and Mrs. Gold had a purpose. Grilling Dane. A good word: It means interrogating . . . but also frying.

Dane is difficult to fry.

"I am conceited, Mr. Gold," she said, flashing her winner's smile. "I admit it. But isn't it better to have a strong ego and face the world with your natural gifts on display than to be some melted candle of a person who never lights up?"

Mr. Gold took refuge slicing the rib roast.

I was impressed. During the week we have pizza or macaroni and cheese. Rib roast! Okay, the potatoes were instant, the broccoli with cheese sauce came in a plastic bag, the biscuits popped out of a cardboard cylinder. Still. They had had to turn on the oven and everything.

"God made the world," said Dane firmly.

Mr. Gold said he had no firm opinions on who made the world.

"You're trying to avoid the issue," Dane accused him. "We are taught to marvel at sunsets and blue skies, aren't we? We're supposed to gasp with pleasure at the sight of scarlet autumn leaves or thrill to the notes of a silvery flute, aren't we? That's beauty, isn't it? Don't people write poems, songs, and essays about beauty?"

Mr. Gold was clearly regretting that he had not prepared more carefully for this encounter. It had not crossed his mind, although they have lived next door for four years, that Dane could debate. That's because he doesn't know that Dane has had to fight with the press all these years.

The press disapproves of beauty pageants. They adore words like *demeaning, degrading,* and *superficial* and they try to get the girls to admit that what they are doing is demeaning, degrading, and superficial. Obviously, if the girl thought that, she wouldn't have entered to start with. Newspaper and TV people will do anything to make pageants look stupid and the contestants look silly. They phrase their questions cleverly.

Not cleverly enough to whip Dane.

"So," said Dane, "shouldn't we also marvel about the beauty of our own bodies?"

"The only thing I marvel about," said Mrs. Gold, "is the extent of the conceit involved."

Dane's smile was blinding. "Mrs. Gold, if Lillie had no faith in herself, could she play the piano onstage, before a packed audience expecting the very best in classical music? You want her to have pride in her ability when it comes to music, don't you?"

"That's different." Mrs. Gold tossed a salad vigorously, trying to come up with why it was different. She had to fall back on her previous phrase. "Beauty pageants are shallow."

"What's shallow about winning?" demanded Dane. "You want Lillie to be a loser? You want her to strive to be mediocre? You want her to wake up in the morning, stretch, and say, 'Oh, goodie. Another day to be ordinary'?"

I noticed something interesting. Lillie, like Dane, was not having broccoli. Some things have a tendency to get stuck. Beauty queens do not risk smiling with a green leaf in their teeth. Beauty queens eat neat vegetables, like carrots, and skip messy vegetables, like spinach. Lillie already knew.

"Of course not!" said Dane. "You want Lillie to get straight A's, be invited to play a piano concerto with a major symphony orchestra, and generally be a star."

"I'm afraid you haven't convinced me. A beauty pageant is degrading."

"Who is degraded? I'm there by choice. Proud to be part of it." Dane smiled sweetly. She has a repertoire of smiles. She sort of leafs through her smile catalog and picks one: *sweet smile, center front.*

Dane dismissed Mr. and Mrs. Gold as she had Thirty-eight. "Lillie, when you were trying on my gowns, I grasped an important aspect of your future and training. You must go with different colors. I'm gentle and blond. I think gentle thoughts when I'm onstage and I go with soft, passive colors. But you are too exotic. You must go with what you are, which is bold and aggressive. You need something in a really stunning purple, or a violent blue."

Lillie nodded eagerly.

"Your posture is so vibrant!" said Dane. "The way you hold your chin is so strong-willed. It's very exciting. It's a gift I don't have, Lillie. You must lean into it."

She was seducing Lillie.

Lillie didn't so much listen as drink. Swallowing every compliment. Thirsting for every sweet nothing.

Her parents were horrified.

And out of ammunition.

They had not known they would need so much.

"Nevertheless," said Mrs. Gold, voice climbing, "the rule stands. If Scottie-Anne isn't in it, Lillie isn't in it."

Thursday, Lillie was back at our house for supper.

I hadn't brought out the permission slip. Nobody in my family even considered the possibility that I might want to enter. Dane does the beauty pageants; I ride in the back.

Lillie was marshaling her forces. She needed my parents on her side. "You see," said Lillie, playing soccer with the remaining green peas on her plate, "I can't enter unless Scottie-Anne does."

I thought my mother might say, *I understand. Of course I'll sign.* Or my father might say, *Scots, do it for Lillie.* Or Dane might say, *With training, and with dedication, Scottie-Anne will be a fine little contestant.*

"Nonsense, Lillie," said Dane. "You don't need Scottie-Anne. One of the best things about pageants is, you pull it off alone. You don't have a buddy in pageants, Lillie. This isn't a relay race. It's not an election with a vice president to take the guff. This is life, Lillie, and you do it alone."

That was enough to scare me off pageants *and* life.

"It's wicked to set that rule," said Dane. "I will speak to your mother and explain how unfair it is."

"My mother isn't interested in your opinion, though, Dane."

My parents ate with the careful, geometric motion of people who would like to do a little people-stabbing with their steak knives, but who have decided to set an example and keep their tempers instead. Mr. and Mrs. Gold had scorned Dane. You don't knock somebody else's kid. I could just imagine what they'd like to say to Mr. and Mrs. Gold: *You blankety, blankety, blank blank blanks . . .*

"Well," said Dane at last. "Then you have to enter, Scottie-Anne. That's the only answer."

48

"No, Dane. I'm against it," said my mother. "Scottie-Anne doesn't want to, do you, dear?"

I didn't want to enter—but I wanted to win! Oh, to be a beauty queen, too!

My mother continued. "I'll talk to Mrs. Gold. I'll explain that Scottie-Anne is just—well—that—"

"That your second daughter is ugly," I said. "That you don't want to see her humiliated onstage. In front of the neighbors. You don't want people to snicker at Scottie-Anne trying to imitate Dane. Because Scottie-Anne wouldn't even be an imitation, would she? She'd be a dud."

"You're not a dud, Scottie-Anne," said my father. "We love you exactly the way you are."

"That's big of you, Father." I never talk back. Father was shocked and silenced.

"Everybody has a special gift, Scottie-Anne," said Dane quickly, "and yours just doesn't happen to be conventional stage-type beauty."

"What is my gift, Dane? Come on, tell me. List my special gifts."

"Don't fight," said Mother desperately. "Let's change the subject."

"You don't want to have to admit out loud that I'm the one without special gifts, huh?"

The table had become a necessity. We were all hanging on to it, staring down into plates or across at candles, anything but saying the truth out loud.

"You're my helper, Scottie-Anne," said Mother.

"You're my good girl, my student, my thoughtful one. You're academic. You're—you're kind, honey. New kids in school always gravitate toward you. You're generous."

"And ugly."

"You're not ugly," said Dane irritably. "You're perfectly acceptable."

Acceptable. Like *nice.* Eighth grade didn't seem so wonderful anymore. I didn't seem so wonderful, either.

"I'm sorry," said Lillie desperately. "My mother is right, Scots. Beauty pageants are ridiculous. It is ridiculous that we are having this discussion at all. Of course, I won't enter."

"What a friendship," I said. "You are willing to sacrifice for me, Lillie. So you don't have to agree with my very own family that I am nothing more than *acceptable.*"

Lillie began to cry. Tears dripped onto her peas. "Mom would never have made that rule if she had realized it would hurt you, Scottie-Anne," she pleaded. "She didn't mean it that way. She just didn't think."

"Who's hurt? You think I've sat through dozens of beauty pageants over the years without noticing that I'm never the one on the runway? I've always accepted that I'm nothing better than acceptable."

My father said to my mother, "I told you this would happen one day, Grace."

"What would happen?" I spat out.

"That your jealousy of me would surface," said Dane.

"I'm not jealous of you!" I cried, getting up from

the table. "I hate you. I hate all of you. But I'm not jealous."

Exit lines are fine.

But then you have to go somewhere. If I ran out of the house, I would have nowhere to go, and it was cold, so I'd have to scramble around and find a coat. Plus it was dark out, and our road has no sidewalks, and it's not easy to walk there at any time, let alone after dark. But if I ran up to my room, slamming doors all the way, they'd talk about how jealous I was, how unfortunate it was that Dane got all the good genes.

Where else do you go, except out of the house or up to your room?

So I very calmly picked up my plate (untouched; for the first time in my life I had eaten the same amount as my sister), took it to the sink, and scraped it all off into the garbage disposal. There was a certain pleasure in listening to the grinding, metallic scream of the blades.

My father came in after me. "Sweetheart," he said, trying to hug me.

I kept my arms full of plates and knives.

"Don't do this," he said.

"I'm not doing a thing. I was born this way."

"I love you," said my father, blocking my return to the dining room. "Scots, answer me."

I said nothing. I was so close to tears and screaming. They had had a glimpse of me, and now it was out. Every pageant would have another element: How do we save poor Scottie-Anne's feelings without depriving Dane of victorious joy?

"I feel rotten," said my father. "Scottie-Anne, I love you," he repeated. Apparently this was the only defense he could come up with for the crime of having one plain and one beautiful daughter. "Listen, Scots. We didn't go through this beauty pageant stuff in order to have a contrast. It just escalated. It's always been so much fun. And Dane hasn't always won. Lots of times she hasn't even placed."

"But I haven't even entered! You never thought of entering me!"

"I can't believe you ever wanted to. You've always been sour on pageants."

"I *don't* want to. I *never* wanted to. I wanted—" But I didn't tell him what I wanted. He should have known without being told. I wanted *other* people to tell me to enter.

Father closed the kitchen door, almost catching my fingers. "You don't go back without telling me you love me."

"What does that have to do with anything?" I said sulkily.

He waited. You don't go to all those pageants without developing an immense capacity for waiting.

"I love you, too," I said unwillingly, and I let him give me a bear hug: a hug to end all hugs. He did love me, with every muscle and fiber of his being.

But love didn't make me beautiful.

5

Dane has her driver's license, but not a car. Every now and then Mother rides to work with her girlfriend and Dane's allowed to take Mother's car to school. This is a treat for both of us, because we are the very first pickup on the school bus route. That means we're standing on the corner at dawn. If we get the car, we also get an extra forty minutes.

As soon as Dane actually got it started (Mother's car is old and pitiful and grinds in agony every morning) she started in on me. "Now, look, Scottie-Anne. I want you to be in the Marsh Mid Princess Pageant. I can give you lots of help. Makeup does wonders. You know that as well as I do. The right dress, the right haircut—you'll be amazed at the transformation. Trust me. Furthermore, you're in luck with this one, because they're only counting beauty as one quarter. That's twenty-five percent, you know."

"No! Is it really?"

"Don't be lippy. And for you, the other three-quarters are a snap. You've got personality, community activity, and academic success all over me."

I said nothing.

"Come on, Scots, please."

"And make a fool of myself like all those pitiful girls in the preliminaries of every pageant you've ever been in? Where only their parents could possibly think they're beautiful? I don't even have that. My parents know damn well I'm not beautiful."

Dane stopped talking. We had to make a left turn across traffic, and traffic is not Dane's strong suit. "Go, Dane," I said.

She sat.

"Go now, Dane, there's tons of space."

"There is not!"

"Dane! Pull out!"

"Scottie-Anne, I'm not into sacrificial deeds, like you. I don't want plastic surgery."

"Twenty minutes later, maybe she'll pull out," I said to the scenery.

Dane, of course, chose the worst possible moment to pull out. People from both directions had to brake and honk. Dane reacted with stupidity, going slower instead of faster, perhaps in the belief that she would not get hit as hard.

"Oh, well," said Dane, "we're alive. Now. About the pageant."

"You just want Lillie to be in it."

"You're right. I want Mr. and Mrs. Gold to have a daughter who is a crowned beauty queen. It would serve them right. They were mean to you, Scottie-Anne. Look how they brought you into the middle of their own private war. Disgusting. This would be your revenge, too."

"I like Mr. and Mrs. Gold."

"They're obnoxious, superior, pseudo-intellectual snobs. Let's bring them down a notch." Dane's grin was tight and wicked. She was taking on the traffic like a race car driver. "They'll have to go to the pageant, you know. They can't skip their own daughter's pageant. They'll have to clap for every girl in it. You can't be rude to your kid's friends' parents." Dane's face was backlit with pleasure. "And I've been in enough pag- eants to know something else, Scottie-Anne. As the tension mounts, and the emcee draws it out, and the competition gets tougher, every single parent on earth gets nervous and sweaty. Every single parent on earth, in the end, wants his or her daughter named the most beautiful, the most talented, and the most desirable.

Mr. and Mrs. Gold are no different. And I want to prove it to them."

Dane actually parallel parked on the first try. This amazing accomplishment had come out of fury, not practice. I had not thought of pure rage as a useful thing.

She had parked adjacent to her school and three blocks from mine. It seemed a statement on my life.

"I've put up with people's rotten attitudes all my life, Scottie-Anne," said Dane. She turned off the ignition lovingly and dropped the key into her purse, where it sank without a trace. "I've had to listen to more crap than most people endure in a lifetime. No adult would dream of going up to a basketball star or an honor roll student and saying, 'Aren't you ashamed of yourself for doing that?' But people walk right up to me! 'Dane, it's so disgusting, why do you do things like that?' Mr. and Mrs. Gold invited us to dinner in order to say that to my face! I hate them. Now, enter the pageant for me, Scottie-Anne, so that Lillie can, too."

We got out of the car.

Dane slammed her door with the triumph of a marching general. "I'm going to thumb my nose at every adult who ever told me, 'Beauty pageants rot.'"

Dane, who always utilizes her time properly, materialized in the middle of my second-period class. Mr. Petrozzi, our science teacher, was lecturing. Mr. Petrozzi is possibly the most rigid human being in education today; there is no rule he bends, ignores, or breaks. One of his rules is that people who interrupt him die.

Of course, when you are Dane, there are no rules. She simply turned on the charm, the smiles, the sweetness, as if he were a judge at the foot of the runway. "Mr. Petrozzi! How wonderful to see you again! Why, I remember this lecture. The old 'Is Japan ahead of us in technology?' catastrophe. Has anything changed since I got the lecture?"

He beamed—Mr. Petrozzi, who never exposes his teeth except to snarl when returning quizzes. "Dane, how nice of you to drop in. Japan's still out in front, I'm ashamed to say. I hope when your class graduates you'll begin to remedy that situation."

"Of course we will," said Dane. "I'll be going into computer technology myself, you know." A serious lie. Dane plans to go into Fame. "I need to whisk my little sister out of class for just a millisecond!" cried Dane, whisking me. "Be right back!"

Nicholas and Eric stared at Dane.

She was wearing a long knit tube of a dress: On the hanger it was a cylinder. On Dane it was no longer a cylinder; today she was going for centerfold. Morgana-Lisa had had an effect.

Boys' eyes widened and became dreamy, covetous, or possibly lustful. They drank her in. Mr. Petrozzi drank her in. The eighth grade girls drank in how the boys reacted, and learned. Tomorrow everybody would be at the mall, testing themselves in knit cylinders.

In the hall, Dane closed the door. It was just us and the wall posters. Voluptuousness vanished and Dane said efficiently, "I filled out your form for you. I called Mother and she's coming over at lunchtime to sign it. Lillie's mother's coming over after work at one P.M. to sign hers. You'll both be ready to pass them in for the assembly, which isn't till two."

"Dane—"

"Read it over. Make sure there are no mistakes."

I looked at the paper. *Marshfield Middle School Princess Encyclopedia Fund-Raising Pageant*, it said. *McKane, Scottie-Anne. Eighth grade.* "Dane! You can't put down *Member: eighth grade choir.* We're all members of the eighth grade choir. It's mandatory."

"You need something under activities, Scottie-Anne. Why don't you have any?"

"Dane! Get off my case! My activity time is used up in the back of the van schlepping you to pageants!"

Dane chewed the ballpoint pen, ink side in her mouth. Good, I thought. Let her get blue lips, let her die in convulsions, see if I care. "We can use that," said my sister. She wrote, *Assistant coach, sister's career.*

"I hate you, Dane."

"You won't when this is over."

"It's over now, Dane. I am not entering."

"I'm entering you. It will build your character. So there."

58

*   *   *

I went back into class, the application form folded into a palm-sized nightmare. My cheeks were hot and I felt sick.

Mr. Petrozzi said, "I hope everything is all right, Scottie-Anne?"

"Yes, thanks." But I was not sure I would be able to keep breakfast down. Too bad I had had so much of it.

Nicholas whispered, "Scots! That's your sister! She's *beautiful*!"

Eric said, "What, you think you're the first one to discover that? You think you're the Christopher Columbus of the teen queen set, maybe?"

"Yeah, Nicholas," said Shannon, "everybody else has been admiring Dane McKane for years."

Nicholas flushed and looked away.

After class he said to me, "You have any leftover wallet pictures, Scots?"

I wrapped my science book in front of my chest. From behind the folds of shoulders and arms and books I said, "You mean of Dane?"

"Well, sure," he said, looking confused. What other girl's wallet photo could he possibly want?

"I can probably get you a photo," I said, thinking it unlikely that anybody would notice one gone from among millions.

"Thanks, Scots!" Nicholas in love. Nicholas with his

first crush. Nicholas, age fourteen, gone gaga over a girl at last. My sister.

I had worn a skirt, which is unusual for me: I am a jeans person. I had snagged my panty hose on a screw some enterprising student had loosened from the chair, and an immense run had filed down my leg. Retreating to the girls' room to throw away the entire panty hose, I struggled to undress in the tiny space between the toilet and the door.

Tasha and Shannon walked in.

I am ambivalent toward Tasha and Shannon. They each have a lot of money to spend and are at ease with boys. I adore boys, but I am not relaxed with them. Whenever I have to talk to a boy, a weird panic envelops me; my voice gets too loud, and my words get stupid. I would like to be friends with Tasha and Shannon and learn how to be easy with boys. On the other hand, I don't like Tasha and Shannon.

"What do you think?" said Shannon. They stayed by the mirrors, obviously checking their faces, as my sister did, for reassurance; or perhaps for pleasure. While I check a mirror to be sure I don't have half a collar sticking up, or buttons misbuttoned, Dane checks for the sheer delight of noticing once more how lovely she is.

Shannon and Tasha are not in Dane's class, but they are of her mind-set.

"I think," said Tasha, "that we better worry about Lillie. She's gorgeous. I never realized it till now. I never thought about us as pageant contestants, is the problem. Lillie has the kind of features that are gorgeous from a distance, too; so audiences will think she's beautiful."

"Mmmm, but you and I look more like Dane. We're blond and slim, too. Whereas Lillie is so extraordinary looking! I've watched all the Miss America and Miss Universe pageants, and you know if you don't keep a scorecard with the states written on them, you can't tell the contestants apart. Lillie's too different. So we're better."

It was going to be interesting to hear backstage pageant cattiness from my classmates. Interesting to see if Shannon and Tasha stayed best friends. To win, one had to better the other.

"What about Scottie-Anne?" said Shannon. "She knows how to walk, and how to smile, and all those tricks you read about in magazines. And you know Dane is going to help her own sister. The judges are supposed to be giving one quarter to each category, and Scottie-Anne could score high in personality, scholarship, and community."

"Come on. Scottie-Anne?"

Shannon laughed. Tasha laughed.

They left the bathroom.

Mother met me in the front lobby, as Dane had instructed, to sign the permission paper. She was coming anyway, because two evenings a week she tutors

English as a second language to the Mexican help at the stable, and she gets her materials through the school. She's always after Dane to tutor a Mexican stable hand, because it would be good for them both, and Dane always replies, "Mother, get a life."

"Hi, darling!" Mother called. She darted over to me. "I'm so proud of you for having the courage to enter the contest." She had her brown bag in her hand. My poor mother has a forty-five-minute lunch hour and crams so many errands into that precious free time that a quick peanut butter and jelly sandwich is the only "lunch hour" she's ever had.

I had been fighting tears all morning. Now the tears were for my mother. Her life was hard. Nobody could pretend otherwise. How she needed the glitter and delight of the pageants! Without them, what would the light of her life be?

"I'm not entering, Mother. Dane just said that in order to get Lillie's mother to sign."

Struggle crossed Mother's face. What does the good parent do? Breathe a sigh of relief that Plain Daughter will not subject us all to public humiliation? Or pretend that Plain Daughter has Potential as Another Beautiful Daughter, hoping that, in this pageant, personality goes a long way?

"What do you want?" said my mother sadly.

I wanted to be beautiful. Or else I wanted the world not to care about beauty so it didn't matter that I was going to stay plain.

I shrugged.

"Dane is showing so much sisterly love," said my mother. "We all acknowledge that Dane isn't as generous and thoughtful as she might be. We all realize that this emphasis over the years on beauty and poise has given Dane—well—conceit. But when she phoned me this morning at work, Scottie-Anne, I was so proud of her! She really cares about you! She wants you to be a winner! She's throwing herself into this!"

She believed what she was saying. My parents always found a way to be proud of Dane. My sister was in fact out to smack the Golds in the face and could not care less if I got squashed in the process.

But the idea of Dane as giver had lit my mother's face.

I pride myself on my mature understanding of life. I always assumed I had had adult thoughts. But at that moment, I had my first one. *I will never be like you, Mother! I will never depend on somebody else's beauty, somebody else's achievements, to carry me through life. I will build my own.*

That hated word.

Build.

But Coach was right.

You had to build.

Mother took the much-folded application from my hand. It was pitiful, torn at two creases, sweat-stained, ink-run. She signed it boldly, with long, straight strikes on the *K* of McKane. "You do what you want, honey," she said. "Father and I love you. You decide what's right for you." She kissed me. "Have to run."

Assembly began. There was an odd, sick tension among the girls. We all had our application forms, and we were all pretending we didn't: as if there was something shameful about the whole business—nobody was going to admit she was entering unless everybody else was entering, too.

The boys had forgotten the whole thing.

Mr. Shippee started with the Pledge of Allegiance, which seemed to last a much shorter time than usual, as if I were being flung up against the pageant, like a ripe fruit against a brick wall.

"Now we have something very important and exciting to discuss," he said.

The girls swallowed and fidgeted.

The boys, who hate important discussions, began pencil duels, stabbing each other's vital parts with the sharp ends, using three-ring notebooks for shields.

"Yale University," said Mr. Shippee, "has a very, very exciting opportunity for our academically minded students."

Every girl in the school stared. What was this gibberish? Yale, involved in a beauty pageant? It seemed unlikely.

Every boy kept stabbing away.

"Yale is offering to the surrounding communities a Russian study program. It is open to any public school student from age fourteen to age eighteen. Some of you eighth graders are fourteen. Every Saturday you will take a special bus into New Haven and spend the day studying Russian language, literature, history, and government. At the end of the year, those who qualify will go on a three-week trip to Russia! Moscow! Leningrad! I have the application forms here. It goes without saying that you must be an excellent student and have the recommendations of all your teachers, and since only eight altogether may go from our entire school system, you are up against serious competition from the high school."

Nobody was listening. Nobody cared about going to Moscow. Nobody wanted to spend Saturday learning Russian. Nobody cared that the world had turned upside down because the Cold War was over and Soviet life was now totally different.

Except me. I shivered with excitement. That language: strange Cyrillic letters. Hissing, mysterious names, like Dostoyevsky. Bolshoi Ballet. Snow that reached rooftops, the Kremlin, spies, and the steppes.

"And speaking of competition," went on Mr. Shippee, "today we are collecting the application forms for the Marshfield Middle School Princess Pageant. I hope we have lots of entrants. It's going to be great fun. Dane McKane, the older sister of our own Scottie-Anne, and the winner of—am I right, Scottie-Anne?— a dozen beauty pageants and the holder of many important state and regional titles, is going to help coach."

I'll take Russian at Yale instead. That will fill my Saturdays, so I won't have time for a beauty pageant. And I can brag about it; I won't look like a pitiful "nice" girl who can't make it otherwise.

All I have to do now is get accepted at Yale University. Hey. No problem. Simple as being Miss Teenage America. I tasted panic. It was metallic, like a new filling in a hurting tooth.

Mrs. Craven walked up the aisle, while girls passed their applications down. She gazed with pleasure at each one and then slipped it into a folder. We stared at the folder as if it were Santa's list of who had been naughty and nice.

I passed Shannon's down. Tasha's. Lillie's.

But not mine.

The relief was overwhelming.

Nicholas said, "Way to go, Scots. Thank God one girl is sane. I told my parents about this dumb pageant thing, and I said, 'Are all girls weird?' My father said, 'Yes, and furthermore, it doesn't change; they stay weird.' My mother said, 'That's okay, all boys have cooties; and that never changes, either!'" Nicholas laughed. How handsome he was! If boys ever entered beauty pageants, he'd win.

Actually, now and then, they do. Sometimes there's a separate division for men. You're always embarrassed for them. Nothing's more pathetic than an eighteen-year-old boy entering a beauty pageant.

I do have an ally, I thought. A boy I adore. Why,

this is just like stories where the moral is: Beauty doesn't count. What counts is being interesting, kind, and—

Shannon brushed up against Nicholas. "You don't have cooties, Nicky. Or if you do, they're really attractive cooties."

Nicholas grinned. Shannon and Nicholas walked up the aisle together.

Wrong.

Beauty does count. It always counts, and it always counts most.

I have never so envied Dane's poise.

That's what it's for, I thought. How not to cry in front of people, how not to break down when you're a loser.

The slant of the auditorium aisle seemed as steep as a ski slope. I leaned forward, trying to get up and out of that horrible room.

"Well, that's that!" said Lillie cheerfully. "We're in now."

"You're in," I said, not even caring if I lost my best friend. "I didn't pass mine in."

Lillie laughed. "Dane knew you'd panic and back out, even though you're really dying to be in it. She gave me a duplicate of yours. I passed it in for you, silly."

"*You what?* What about what *I* want? What about my mother's signature?"

"Dane forged it, of course."

"Wonderful. Beauty queen as forger."

"Scottie-Anne," said my best friend gently. "You're taking this all too seriously. It's just a game. We're just going to have fun."

6

If there's a test, and you don't bother to study, and then you fail, you say to yourself, "Oh, well. I could have gotten an A if I'd bothered." It's comforting. Spares you the trouble of studying, but keeps you from feeling lousy.

I can only assume that is why I didn't storm up to Mrs. Craven, grab the forged application back, and rip it to shreds in front of Lillie and Dane.

When I failed miserably in the pageant, I could shrug. *After all, I didn't enter. They entered me. It's their fault.*

There was a soccer game on the west field, and a field hockey game on the east field, and tennis on the courts beyond the row of pines.

I wandered, checking out one game and then the others. Usually I travel in a pack; I dislike being by myself in public. But that afternoon I didn't mind and just walked back and forth over the fields, listening to the screaming whistles of refs.

Lillie was at her piano lesson; she goes into New Haven, her instructor comes out from New York City. That's the level Lillie's reached: They come to her.

Who comes to me? I thought. Why should they?

There are days when you are full of school, of friendship and laughter. But nothing existed inside my flesh except self: I was thick with me. The playing fields seemed to lie at a great distance; teams and spectators were strangers. Their sounds were foreign languages.

I watched, but wasn't drawn in; listened, but didn't hear. It was the ultimate shyness. I went outward only; nothing came in.

I grew all afternoon, adding thoughts like extra pounds. Who was this girl whose body I inhabited? Whose heart pounded with joy at the thought of her *own* first evening gown? Whose heart raced for her *own* matching dyed slippers? Whose heart trembled for her *own* lights, camera, action, and applause?

Who was this girl, who wanted to be Marsh Mid Princess, after all?

*   *   *

I got home late, so bulky with myself I had the feeling I might not fit in the door. My *self* had expanded. I was as filling as a thick milk shake.

The house felt strange and cold.

I found my mother leaning up against the cabinets in the kitchen, grocery bags all over the counters, not yet emptied. "Mother? Are you all right?"

She truly looked drained, as if some terrible household vampire had sucked her dry of life and laughter. "Just tired, honey," said my mother.

"I'll put away the groceries," I said quickly.

She nodded. Even her nod lacked energy. She had faded like cloth in the sun. "I'll make supper," I added.

She nodded.

"Mom, are you all right?"

"It's Friday, honey. I always need to wind down a little on a Friday evening."

I put groceries away. She's a shift manager at Elson's, where they make plastic tubes and bags for hospital use. She walks up and down the assembly lines, checks, helps, encourages, teaches, assigns breaks.

"I usually go shopping with your father Thursday nights at Stop N Shop, but we couldn't manage it, so I had to go after work today. For some reason it sapped me. Aisles seemed to stretch on forever. I felt as if I had to go to Siberia to find a gallon of milk. There seemed to be at least six thousand shapes of pasta." She managed a laugh. "Guess I'm pretty tired when I can't decide between elbow noodles and rotelli."

71

I was putting away the macaroni. "You chose rotelli," I said. "Want me to make tomato sauce?"

She shook her head. "Just open a jar of spaghetti sauce. It's going to take everything I have to boil the water."

"I'll do it, Mother, don't worry about it. Why don't you watch TV while I fix supper?"

She shook her head again. "Have to turn the knob, Scottie-Anne. I think it's beyond me."

We giggled.

Dane came flying down the stairs. "Look, Mother!" she cried, waving a thick envelope. "I got the information back from Miss Teenage America! I'm in the preliminaries! Here are the dates!"

My mother took the packet with a cry of delight, mindless as a songbird's. Tiredness fled. She and Dane hovered over the pictures and forms, eyes bright, lips wet. Among the brown paper grocery bags, their faces gleamed. Equally beautiful.

Perhaps excitement is beauty.

Mrs. Gold had demanded, "Whose pageant is it, anyway? Dane's or your parents'?" That was the sticking point for her—whose idea was it? If it was the parents' idea, it was wrong; it forced an innocent child to market her body. If it was the girl's idea, it was also wrong; parents had taught the wrong values about self-worth.

Something in pageants makes my mother sparkle. She does pour herself and Dane into those pageants—

but pageants give it back. Work doesn't give it back. Shopping doesn't. Making supper doesn't.

How I wanted to give my mother the pleasure only Dane had given till now. To shine for her.

And see her shine back.

Dane is smart.

You can't get away from that.

She didn't open the first practice of the Marsh Mid Princess Pageant wearing her many-layered gold and silver gown. She didn't wheel in a table overflowing with trophies.

She brought three videos. Laughing, at ease, she chattered to the twenty-one of us contestants. "Now, you'll want to see me in my first teenage pageant. Of course, I'd been in plenty of juvenile pageants and won plenty of ribbons and hardware. That's slang for medals. But I'd been with eight- or ten-year-olds. I had never worn high heels before. Never had a floor-length gown before. Certainly never a strapless gown. Here, for the first time, I'm in a pageant up against girls as old as eighteen."

She fast forwarded, stopping momentarily to show teenagers in fabulous, sexy gowns slit to the thigh and teasing at the bosom. They were glamorous. They were stylish. They were beautiful.

"Okay, now, pay attention, here," Dane said. "See me peeking behind the curtain because I'm next? There I come. Out to the center of the stage. Now I trip over a guy wire I forgot was there and go down on both knees. Now I can't get up again, because my skirt is tight and I have no idea how to maneuver. I'm still trying to smile. See how I turn to the cameras and show my teeth, like an insane person? The emcee tries to help, except the cord to his mike yanks him backward. See the color guard trying to decide whether to hand the flag to the guy next to him and go pick me up, or pretend he doesn't notice?"

The girls were laughing hysterically.

There was Dane, crawling around on the stage, trying to remove herself from an invisible wire. She resembled nothing so much as a fish on a line, flopping for air. When she was finally erect, one shoe had come off. Dane couldn't get her foot back in and hopped around in circles, shoving her toe at an escaping shoe.

The film was relentless.

It showed everything.

The audience clapped for Dane, as in basketball you clap for a downed player gamely leaving the court. The emcee said, "Well! That was quite an entrance, Number Seventeen. Ladies and gentlemen, we're a little better acquainted with Dane McKane than with some of our other contestants. Dane is thirteen years old, from Marshfield. I guess this is the best Marshfield has to offer this year!"

The girls were horrified. "Dane, he didn't really say that!"

"Sometimes emcees are really cruel. I don't know if

they think they're being funny, or if they don't know how to fill the time with nicer patter, or if they really get a kick out of being mean. But there's not much you can do. If you kick the emcee in the shins, you lose points."

Everybody laughed.

"Now, this is a video of a really weird pageant I was in last year; it was an all–New England pageant, partially sponsored by the Yellow Cookware Company. We were required to set tables as our talent, cook meals involving Yellow Cookware, and give a Yellow Cookware theme party. This is me at our house, surrounded by my Yellow Cookware, laughing happily. Actually, I'm laughing hysterically, because my cake has failed for the third time, and we are about to lift it out of the oven, in its Yellow Cookware, a cake with the flavor and texture of tan glue. Here's the table, and you can see that for my theme I chose wildflowers. Unfortunately, I had to pick the flowers two days early, because I was also in the school play at that time and had rehearsals. So my wildflowers are the little dead things you see leaning out of jelly jars."

The middle school girls were laughing so hard they could barely sit up to look at the rest of the videos.

"I've lost more pageants than I've won," said Dane. "But what I have really won is poise. I am sixteen and I can handle anything. A pageant is a solo. There are no team members to carry the ball for you. There's no supporting cast and no prompter. There's no piano, no director, and no chorus. You go out there and you're on your own. It's scary. But I promise you, you never trip over the wire a second time. You learn."

Dane stood tall and slender before us. The flopping fish of that first pageant was not visible. A beautiful, accomplished woman looked down at scrawny, underdone middle school girls. "Here's the last video. This is the Eastern States Star Pageant. I was up against the four winners from each of eighteen states. There are some very beautiful women on this stage."

The video was a breathtaking sweep of loveliness.

You could not imagine what would make one better than the other.

Could not imagine being a judge and separating out these girls.

Dane fast forwarded to herself.

The girls leaned toward the screen.

A girl as fragile as spun gold stood before a crowd of hundreds. Her gown was white, threaded with more gold. Elaborate, tumbling curls wrapped her fair face like a sunrise. When she walked down the runway, she smiled so lovingly you could feel her affection. She extended her arms to the crowd, and the picture was momentarily blocked off, as rows of spectators stood to applaud.

Now she walked in the other direction, turning gracefully to face each section of the admiring audience. At the stage edge, she wafted a kiss into the applause and waved good-bye.

"I won that," said Dane matter-of-factly. "I was the Star."

Dane knew better than to brag about her body. Didn't explain that she knew how to milk a crowd. *I was the Star.*

What did any of us want, except to be the Star? Face that camera. Hear that clapping. Wear that crown.

Because those three—camera, clapping, and crown—equal stardom.

We ceased to be twenty-one giggling sixth, seventh, and eighth grade girls. We were in competition. Trying to have Dane. To be Dane.

Only I knew that Dane was taken. She was grooming Lillie, and if the rest of us got ulcers or smallpox, she'd be glad.

Saturday Dane said that Lillie and I could go to the pageant rehearsals and watch her. Lillie and I would pick up pointers and get a better feel. I said my feel was sour, and the only pointer I wanted was one to stab Dane with.

Lillie said crossly, "Scottie-Anne, Dane and I did what's best for you. You would never have forgiven yourself if you didn't try."

"I'm never forgiving myself for not going back up to Mrs. Craven and snatching my application form back," I said.

It was an unseasonably warm day, and Dane had decided to wear her dance costume up rather than change. The costume was supposed to be western. A Connecticut pageant's idea of western has to be seen to be believed.

Each cowgirl (like Dane) wore red silk shorts with a white silk blouse, white tights with red spangles, and red calf-high boots with taps. Plus each girl carried a white jump rope with red tassels. This was supposed to be a lasso. On the stage were three large, flat wooden cows, black and white, around which the girls danced, and over which they flipped. Girls incapable of cow-flipping twirled their lassos and tried to look western.

"Father can't drive us," said Dane, "and Mother needs her car. So I'm driving the van. Scots, sit up front and tell me the turns."

"You're driving the van? We stay home, Lillie. Dane in the van is death."

"Once I'm on the turnpike I'm fine," protested Dane. "I'll stay in the slow lane. Scottie-Anne, you shift for me."

"Wait a minute," said Lillie. "It takes two of you to drive?"

"She's good at neutral," I explained, "but she hasn't gotten first, second, third, or fourth down."

Lillie paled, which showed she had retained some reasoning ability. Luckily, Father had backed into the driveway, so we didn't have to find reverse. I shoved. Dane pumped. The van bucked. Lillie's eyes swiveled, searching out contenders for the right-of-way. Dane hunched over the wheel, looking straight ahead.

78

"They gave her a license," I told Lillie, "because she hypnotized the Motor Vehicle Bureau with her beauty."

"I believe you," said Lillie nervously. "Beauty is the only thing Dane has to offer as a driver. But can beauty fend off tractor-trailers?"

Dane started the approach to the turnpike at twenty-five miles per hour. Since nobody obeys speed laws in Connecticut, she was going to have to merge with a thousand trucks going seventy-five. "Dane, step on the gas!" shrieked Lillie.

Dane whipped her speed up to thirty.

"No!" I yelled. "Let that truck by!"

"Not yet!" screamed Lillie. "There isn't—"

Dane pulled out. There was no crunch. "We're not even dead," said Lillie.

"I lead that kind of life," explained Dane. "People just move over for me."

Lillie started to laugh until she saw that Dane was serious. Dane was not threatened by tons of surging metal. People moved over for her.

This remained true for quite a few miles. True until the high school sponsoring the pageant appeared in the distance. Dane, thrilled to have arrived, forgot she had another stoplight to go. "Dane, it's red."

"What is?"

"The light."

"What light?"

Brakes and Lillie screamed.

"Oh, that light," said Dane, and she giggled like a maniac.

"It's beyond me why Father and Mother let you drive."

"Because they don't know you're doing the shifting. Lillie, stop your noise. We aren't hit. Don't make such a big deal out of it."

The drivers of three of the four vehicles that had almost clobbered us shook fists and drove around us. One did not. The driver's door opened. The passenger's door opened. Out got two big, ugly brutes. Lillie whimpered. Dane rolled down her window and leaned out.

"Watch this, Lillie," I said. "This is what Dane really learned from all her beauty pageants."

Dane hopped down to the pavement. "I'm really sorry," she said to the advancing killers. Sun glittered off her red and white spangles. "I'm just a terrible driver! I'm borrowing my daddy's car, and I can hardly manage such a big old van! You're just such an excellent driver, to miss me like that. You're wonderful."

They ceased to be killers. No longer brutes, they were broad-shouldered young men face-to-face with a princess. They absorbed her, from her frothy golden hair to her scarlet dancing boots. "Wow," they whispered. And, more eagerly, "Say! Hi, there!"

Dane beamed at them. Danger over, she began backing into the van.

The first guy was already in love. "My name's Zach.

I go to college up here. Are you—uh—what campus are you on?" He was practically on his knees. Any minute now he would thank her for ignoring the red light.

"You're so sweet," said Dane. "I don't live around here. I'm on my way to a stage rehearsal."

We might possibly have stayed in that intersection for hours, while Dane flirted, Zach fell in love, and Lillie took notes, except that other drivers, possibly with places to go, were less impressed with Dane and were leaning on their horns and yelling obscenities out their windows.

Dane hopped back in the car. "Times like this," she said to Lillie, "I really wish I had dimples. Where's first gear, Scottie-Anne?" I shoved it into first. We throttled right out into traffic, which did not hit us this time, either.

"Bye, Zach!" Dane cried, waving and smiling. At least she remembered to use the pedals. I shifted and steered. We crossed the street, entered the parking lot, parked without denting anybody, and turned off the engine. "Thank God," whispered Lillie.

Dane hopped out. She smoothed her tiny silk cowgirl outfit and admired herself. "God?" repeated Dane. "Naah. It was me."

7

❋

The girls worked on their routine for two solid hours.

The manager of the pageant had worked up a rough draft for the program. She was double-checking facts with every girl.

Lillie and I sat in the back. The manager sat two rows ahead of us, calling each girl down. "Jill!" she screamed in a thin voice, as if through a straw.

Jill ceased practicing, vaulted off the stage, and bounced toward the manager. Jill was a tiny thing— almost a miniature person—with remarkably white skin, as if she had not left her house since birth. Her hair was so brown she gleamed. "Maybe she's part otter," whispered Lillie.

"Jill," twirped the manager, "what year were you Connecticut's Junior Miss?"

"Last year, of course." Jill, quite irritated that anybody on earth could have forgotten such a vital fact, snatched the program. "No, no, I placed *first* in the Dance Educators of America Miss Broadway Competition. And *second* in the Fred Astaire International Tap Dancing Competition. And be sure to put down that I get straight A's. I tutor physics and chemistry. And you've left out that I was Miss Hartford Chamber of Commerce, Miss Litchfield Fair, and Miss High School of Connecticut."

Lillie was awestruck. She leaned forward and interrupted them. "Wow, I'm so impressed, Jill. You get straight A's and tutor physics and chemistry? I have to tell my mother; she'll think so much more highly of beauty pageants."

I shrank back.

Jill glared at us. "Who the hell are you? Strangers aren't allowed in here. What are you doing at our rehearsal?"

"My mother's the high school principal here," snapped Lillie, proving that she could lie with the best of them. "We're waiting for our ride home. Now, why is a physics and chemistry tutor entering a beauty pageant?"

"I cannot imagine," said Jill, "who misinformed you that this is a beauty pageant. This is a scholarship contest."

My eyes flew to the stage, where twenty-eight nearly naked girls did flips over their white jump ropes. (Pardon me. Lassos.)

"There is a five-thousand-dollar scholarship at stake here," said Jill crisply, "and I will be winning it."

Jill bounded back to the stage.

"Next routine!" cried the instructor onstage.

"They do another dance?" asked Lillie.

"In scholarship pageants they aren't called dances," I said. "They're called physical fitness routines."

"Kerry!" screamed the manager.

The next girl to leave the stage was taller, heavier, and far less agile than Jill. Her red silk shorts bulged at the thighs, and her bosom bounced painfully beneath its gap-buttoned blouse. Out of breath even before she reached the manager, she sagged into a chair and panted loudly.

"Kerry, I don't have any previous titles for you," said the manager, pencil poised to jot down a list of them.

"I've never entered anything before," said Kerry.

Lillie shuddered. "Kerry's up against girls like that Jill and your sister?" she whispered. "How does she dare?"

"Probably didn't know. See, they bill these things as scholarship contests, and lots of times girls actually believe that. And they need the money for college, and

84

they figure, *Oh, I can go onstage for an hour.* They don't know that every girl here has already passed the scholarship requirement. From here in, it's all beauty and talent. I know Jill pretty well from other contests she and Dane have been in. Jill didn't recognize me, but I didn't expect her to. Pageant contestants never recognize anybody but the competition. Jill is tough stuff. Last year she did a combination tap dance and baton routine that was out of this world. Queer. But impressive."

Lillie said, "I've never danced a step in my life."

"Start now. See if your mother will be happy to give you jazz, tap, and ballet lessons."

Kerry returned to the stage. Too out of shape to leap up the way Jill had, but finding the steps blocked with sound equipment, she heaved herself up, rear end first. *Ample* rear end first.

"Kerry," said the dance instructor, "when you need practice the most of anybody, why dawdle? Jill, show Kerry how this step is done. Kerry, try to pay attention. We are tired of slowing to your pace."

"Pace?" snorted another girl. "Sitting is the only pace Kerry has."

Kerry flushed, staggering clumsily in Jill's wake.

"The whole routine is going to be ruined if Kerry can't do better than this," whined the other girl. "I mean, Kerry, what are you even doing in this pageant?"

"Be quiet!" shouted Dane. "Kerry's in the pageant

to get the scholarship." Dane flounced out of line and put her arm around Kerry's thick waist. "Here, Kerry," she said gently. "Like this." Together they executed the step several times, Dane nudging Kerry into place by hip or hand.

"Dane's so kind," said Lillie dreamily.

"She isn't kind. She wants the Miss Friendship Award, and furthermore, if they lose a girl at this stage, the routines have to be rechoreographed."

Lillie glared at me. "You have a terrible attitude toward your sister, Scottie-Anne."

"I know my sister, Lillie. You're the one developing an attitude. You're taking this too seriously. Just yesterday you told me it's only a game. A game worth a forgery, of course, but a game."

Lillie watched as if seeing Princess Diana getting married. It was already no game to Lillie.

In the school office I picked up an application form for the Yale Russian program. After the routine fill-ins for place of birth and social security number, each question was followed by enough space for serious essays. I considered answering truthfully.

"Why do you want to participate in this program?" *Because I don't want to be in a beauty pageant, of course.*

"What special gifts will you bring to Yale?" *The ability to sit through anything, no matter how boring.*

"Are you fluent in other languages?" *Yes. Beauty-speak.*

Dane has certainly never told the truth on her applications. She's close. But not quite truthful. I'm willing to bet, for example, that Jill does not tutor physics and chemistry on a daily basis. Probably once helped a kid study for a test.

"Why do you want to participate in this program?" Yale asked me. After considerable thought, I wrote, *My school is absorbed by athletic events and beauty pageants. I feel an intense need to reach beyond the restrictive, old-fashioned entertainments of my friends. The chance to immerse myself in academic enlightenment is what I have been dreaming of.*

"What special gifts will you bring to Yale?"

A lifelong passion for Soviet-American relationships, I wrote, making a note to read something about Russia before I arrived at Yale for the first time.

"Are you fluent in other languages?"

My school, being rural and underfunded, does not offer foreign language study to lower grades. It is generous and thoughtful of Yale University to extend such an opportunity to the communities who look to New Haven for intellectual guidance.

Beauty pageant emcees swallow that kind of thing.

Perhaps Yale would.

Perhaps Yale wouldn't.

"Look!" screamed Shannon, waving a newspaper in our faces. "Look at this advertisement."

Miss Connecticut SuperTeen Pageant
Official Preliminary to
The National USA Miss SuperTeen
of America Pageant

no performing talent required!

You could have the fun, glamour, and excitement of competing in a most prestigious teenage pageant! If you are between fourteen and nineteen, never married, and a U.S. citizen, you may qualify to compete in the state pageant this winter! Contestants will compete in sportswear, poise and personality, and evening gown! Along with her expense-paid trip to the nationals in Myrtle Beach, South Carolina, our state winner will receive a host of thrilling prizes, including travel, wardrobe, cash, and scholarships! All girls interested in the fun and excitement of competing for the title must write, including snapshot, bio, and phone number . . .

"Let's enter!" screamed Shannon. "Who'll enter with me?"

"I will!" cried Tasha.

Lillie whispered to me, "Should I enter it? I need practice, too. We could carpool."

"Stay clear. It's worthless. Let them go."

"Why is it worthless?" said Shannon, overhearing me.

I shrugged.

"You've been to all this stuff. Come on, tell. What's wrong with it?"

"It's a franchise, like mufflers for cars, or fried chicken. They're earning a living, and it happens to be through beauty pageants. There won't be any glamour or excitement except what you provide. And it'll be very expensive. You'll have to pay a steep entrance fee. You'll have to buy advertising in their program. You'll have to use their photographer for your official photo to go into the program. Furthermore, if you do win, even though they pay your airfare, they don't pay your family's, and they don't pay your hotel bill or your food or your living expenses for the time you're there. And you've got to provide your own sponsors for the national, too. It would cost more money than the national winner would win."

The giveaway line is "no performing talent required." That means any girl who forks over the money can enter. Or, as Dane puts it, not only is no talent *needed,* nobody *with* talent will compete.

"I don't care," said Shannon. "I need practice. It'll be a good pageant to make mistakes in, like that wire-tripper your sister showed us. It won't matter, and I can learn poise there."

Shannon and Tasha decided to enter.

My parents had moved their chairs close together, hovering over a single sheet of paper, sharing a pen.

Dane frowned at Father. "What are you and Mother fussing over?" she said.

"Scottie-Anne's Yale application," said Father. "It's pretty scary. We have to write an essay of our own. Plus, we have to promise that if she's accepted, we'll get her there and she won't drop out."

"Yale!" repeated Dane. "She's in eighth grade!"

"But I'm brilliant," I said, "and they have a vacancy in the freshman year and called me up and asked—"

"Shut up," said Dane. "Father, what does Yale have to do with anything?"

"It's a Russian studies program for fourteen- to eighteen-year-olds in the state of Connecticut. Yale feels that the United States is sorely lacking in addressing the need for knowledgeable Soviet specialists and Russian speakers. In the decades to come, we—"

"That has nothing to do with Scottie-Anne," said Dane sharply.

"She's applying. It's every Saturday till spring, and if she stays with the course, she gets to go to Moscow and tour Russia for three weeks."

"She's in eighth grade!" cried Dane. "How could she deserve a trip to Russia? She's never done anything!"

Father looked up. "Dane, what's the matter with you?"

"She's jealous!" I said gleefully.

My sister's beautiful face curled up like old paper. "You're not even a straight-A student, Scottie-Anne. Why would Yale University want you contaminating their halls?"

"Jea-lous," I sang.

Mother said, "Jase, I think we'd better write a rough draft of our essay first, don't you? What if we misspelled a word?"

"Yale would assume it's bailing out the lower classes," said Dane. "Not that it matters. Yale doesn't stoop as low as Scottie-Anne."

Father looked up a second time. He said, "Danish, old cheese, it's be-polite-to-your-sister time. We have only one reliable car, and that's the van, and if we sign a promise to get Scottie-Anne to New Haven, we'll keep that promise, and if you're rude, you're the one without a ride to *your* practices. Which would disqualify you from Miss Teenage America. Clear?"

My sister summoned all the false sweetness learned in years of pageantry. "Yes, Father. You're right, of course. I'm so sorry, Scottie-Anne."

She loaded the dishwasher. I scrubbed pots. "Scottie-Anne," she said, too softly for Mother and Father to hear, "you get in my way, you bother a single minute of my schedule, and you're dead. Clear?"

We had never been at war before.

She had been the queen and I had been her slave runner-up.

Oh, how good to have ammunition! "I plan to be Marsh Mid Princess as well as Russian scholar," I told my sister. "And if you get in *my* way, or bother a single minute of *my* schedule, Dane, *you're* dead. Clear?"

91

8

"Lillie, you nauseate me," said her mother. "One week ago, you never said anything catty about anybody. Now it's all you ever say."

"Now I see the other girls more clearly," said Lillie. "It's part of being in a pageant; you learn how to judge."

Mrs. Gold moaned. "And you, Scottie-Anne? You are actually glad that my daughter and your sister forged a signature to get you in? I have no faith in anybody anymore."

92

"It wasn't a real forgery," said Lillie. "Mrs. McKane had already signed an application. We just re-signed."

"But how are you and Dane managing to live in the same house?" said Mrs. Gold. "Now that you are at war?"

"Actually, it's kind of fun."

"War is fun?"

"Yes. Who would have guessed it, with all this hype in favor of peace? Every morning when I get up, I can just hardly wait to draw blood."

"I am appalled," said Mrs. Gold.

"It's scary," said Lillie. "They've always been civil to each other. Dane wins the trophies while Scottie-Anne sits quietly in the backseat, and—"

"It's the old backseat every time, isn't it?" said Mrs. Gold. "Sooner or later, the peasants rebel. They want the front seat for themselves." Mrs. Gold and I laughed like maniacs, but Lillie remained blank. That stopped my laughter. Who wants to be right about *that* guess— eighth grade and my best friend is forty?

Lillie said, "But the real question is, what shall I play for my talent? Nobody in junior high wants to hear Beethoven. My piano piece has to be a crowd pleaser. Dane explained that you cannot go out there and do what you want. You have to do what the audience wants. Dane says what I need is a piece that is both simple and smashing, during every note of which I will look graceful."

Mrs. Gold said perhaps the instructor from New

York City would like to help. She was sure he had a great deal of experience at junior high beauty pageant preferences. He would be fascinated to hear that this year's goal was a piece that would show off Lillie's knees to advantage.

"Mom, don't be snide."

"Me? Snide? How about you two? What was that I just heard you say about poor little Shannon?"

"Shannon," said Lillie scornfully, "plays chord organ. The kind where you play the melody with one finger of one hand, and it pokes in the chords and the rhythms. Can you believe she's actually going to play that on a stage? As if it's music? Hah! And Tasha! She's going to sing. The chorus teacher is going to help her learn something. Tasha—who couldn't sing her way out of a paper bag." Lillie tossed her head. When she was done tossing she sat as Dane had shown her: upright, but not bolt upright; shoulders at ease, but not slumped. Your basic beautiful-girl-at-rest posture. Then Lillie wet her lips and smiled, as for a camera in the distance.

Mrs. Gold moaned again. She muttered something about needing a blindfold and perhaps earplugs to get through the next few months. "Oh, Scottie-Anne," she said. "And to think that all these years I believed in your sanity. Oh, well. Now, what's your talent, Scottie-Anne?"

Lillie opened her eyes very wide (to dazzle an assortment of invisible judges), blinked as if scooping snow off the sidewalk with her lashes, and awaited my answer with the perky interest each beauty contestant must have in the others, if she is to win Miss Amity.

"*Aaaaaahhhhhhhh!*" screamed Mrs. Gold. "I apologize, Scottie-Anne. I can't believe I said that out loud. I actually asked you what your talent is. As if every girl has but one. As if it matters. As if the girl who cannot twirl a baton is ready for the bird feeder."

I smiled forgivingly, but my heart pounded. All these years we had worried about Dane's lack of talent. But the truth, of course, is that I—like my sister—basically have no talents. . . .

All day long, in school, I tested myself for talents. Glancing through books, eyeing blackboards, listening to answers, I kept a mental eye out for stage talent.

Math. No.

English. No.

History. No.

Science. No.

Music. No.

Gym. No.

Art. No.

Computer. No.

What was I going to do in public, on a stage, in front of lights and camera, to get people to clap for me?

"Now, girls," said Mrs. Craven, "we must all have a community activity. There are two ways to handle this. Either each girl individually begins a genuine contribution to town, school, church, or club; or, as a group, we think of a special something to do together!" It was obvious from the way she clasped her hands in front of her which she wanted, so Shannon cried, "A special something together, Mrs. Craven! Something you help us with! You have such good ideas!"

Mrs. Craven beamed at her. "Thank you, Shannon. But first, ideas from the group!"

"The soup kitchen needs volunteers," said Dane, who hadn't been there in months.

"I don't know," said Shannon dubiously. "Don't yucky people go there? Smelly and all?"

"Yes," said Dane, who is not fond of yucky people, either.

"If everybody knows how to knit," suggested Mrs. Craven, "we could participate in the Caps for Kids Christmas Gift Program!"

Nobody knew how to knit. Nobody wanted to know how to knit. Nobody could believe Mrs. Craven seriously believed that twenty-one middle school girls were about to meet afternoons to knit one, purl one.

Shannon said, "Maybe we could patrol the school grounds on a sunny day and pick up trash. I saw soda cans over by the fence."

"I don't want to do anything icky," said Tasha.

"I want to do something indoors," said Jodie. "We could make posters for MADD or for Just Say No."

"We could hand out condoms," said Tasha.

Mrs. Craven said, "What? I must have misunderstood you, Tasha, dear."

Tasha smiled sweetly. "I'm sure you did," she agreed gravely.

"I vote for individual projects," I said. "Otherwise, we're not competing. In a group activity, we'll be equal."

Everybody glared at me.

Lillie giggled. "Scottie-Anne, you just lost your chance at being elected Miss Most Beloved of All."

I took a deep breath. I was terrified. Of all the things I have never been, a leader is what I most have never been. "I have another suggestion," I said, shivering. "Times have changed. This isn't the nineteen fifties, where all a girl could do was, say, twirl a baton, or play a Chopin waltz. Nowadays girls are terrific at thousands of things. Like you, Janet. You designed a computer game last year that the elementary school is using for math facts. And you, Laurie. You designed the mural that the art classes painted on the cafeteria wall. And Jodie, you reupholstered your older brother's car with his T-shirt collection."

They were staring at me, unable to guess where I was going.

Dane knew. She was white with fury. But this was war, after all, and if I was going to win, I had to outwit both Dane and Lillie at the same time. "So my suggestion," I said, drawing my sister's blood, "is that for talent, we can either go onstage, the way Lillie will,

97

and play the piano live and in person . . . or we can videotape what we've done elsewhere, and play the tape for our talent!"

Dane shot out of her chair. She was trying not to spit, trying to retain a little beauty queen grace. "Some of us have worked for years! Have taken lessons! Practiced daily! Disciplined ourselves! *We* are the ones who—"

"A brilliant idea," said Mrs. Craven. "We'll do it."

Dane stood very thin, very hard. "I think there should be a vote."

"Nonsense," said Mrs. Craven. "Since when are beauty pageants a democracy? I'm in charge, it's a good suggestion, and we'll do it. Thank you, Scottie-Anne. I am sure you are back in the running for Miss Most Beloved of All, although we aren't having such a category. It was my experience, in becoming Miss Georgia, that that sort of category leads to backstage politicking that can only be described as slimy."

The look Dane gave me also could only be described as slimy. Because if the talent did not have to be onstage, Lillie did not necessarily have it cornered.

"By the way, Dane," said Mrs. Craven, "what pageant are you presently rehearsing for?"

Finding a white-toothed smile from somewhere in the depths of her self-control, Dane said, "USA–T.E.N.E. It's very famous. Teens Excel in National Events. It's a scholarship program. I'll get five thousand dollars if I win."

"Five thousand dollars!" screamed everybody, impressed to the bottom of their sweatsocks.

I was not impressed. My parents had invested at least twice that much in video equipment, cameras, and film alone. Add in designer gowns, professional training, dance lessons, and a custom van . . . five thousand dollars is a roll of quarters.

"You'll win, won't you?" said Shannon reverently. Shannon looked at Dane the way younger girls do look at beauty queens: with worship and admiration.

Dane ducked her head modestly. "I think I have a chance, Shannon," she said.

They were as impressed by her modesty as by the five thousand dollars. Little did they know.

The next day was Friday. I had never felt so TGIF. The first week of pageant rehearsals had been so frightening that even I, who had known what was coming, how much work was involved, how many hours of learning group numbers, learning to walk, and so forth, felt daunted. And, of course, now that Dane hated me, and Lillie was hostile, too, I was not exactly surrounded by friends.

Class had been particularly exhausting: We were beginning the second marking period and each teacher had taken a new breath and gotten off to a running start. In sports, field hockey and soccer had ended; basketball was beginning. I can never remember which end of the court my team has. Basketball isn't a sport that I give any time or concentration. Twice last year I totally embarrassed myself by making points for the opposite team. So basketball season is not my favorite.

And for my family, this weekend was Dane's T.E.N.E. Pageant. All preliminaries would be Saturday night: talent, bathing suit, evening gown, and interview. Sunday afternoon, for the finals, enough of our family and friends were going that we chartered a bus to pick up at the high school. All four grandparents were driving in and three cars of neighbors. Even Mr. and Mrs. Gold were attending. They said it was time they knew firsthand what a beauty contest consisted of.

Dane and I were not speaking to each other.

She was so angry over the video concept that she trembled. I could tell when she was thinking about it by looking at her skin.

Interestingly enough, though, Dane's appetite had begun to show itself somewhat. When I started to remark on this at dinner, my mother stepped on my foot to silence me. Afterward she said, "Scottie-Anne, I took Dane to a doctor. I had had a long talk with the doctor ahead of time; she's a nutrition counselor for adolescents. She said Dane is not anorexic, but we have to be careful. When I took Dane there the doctor was categorical. She said to Dane, 'You are endangering your future babies, your future bone structure, and your future muscle strength, Dane. I have called your school nurse. You are going to be weighed in the nurse's office every morning before class begins. I want you to put on ten pounds.' Dane, of course, said if she put on ten pounds she couldn't wear her gowns. I said I had talked to Micharde-Miquelle about it, and they would adjust the gowns if necessary, so that wasn't a problem. The doctor said, 'If you lose any weight from now on in, Dane, you will start psychiatric treatment, and although I myself am a beauty contest winner, and paid for a year of medical school on a pageant scholarship, and I sympathize with you, the psychiatrist is going to blame beauty pageants and insist that you drop them.' "

I nearly dropped myself.

Mother nodded. "Dane said she'd eat, and she's eating."

"Not one of her talents," I said. "Mother, is that one reason you've been so tense lately?"

She nodded. "Your father and I read an article in *Woman's Day* about anorexia, and we panicked. We've set up guidelines, and I feel good about it."

My waffling, nervous parents were actually coming down hard.

"One of the rules, Scottie-Anne," said my mother, "is that you don't tease Dane about food. You don't talk about it. Period."

"Promise."

"That's my good girl." My mother's eyes filled with tears, and she hugged me suddenly, and so hard. "I've never had to worry about you," she said. "I've never gotten sick with nerves over you. You're always my sturdy one. But you never wanted to be sturdy, did

101

you? You wanted to be Cinderella, too. Oh, Scottie-Anne, I don't feel as if your father and I did very well."

"You did great," I said. Her tears horrified me.

"I'm nervous over you, now."

"Why?"

"Yale," she said. "I want you to get in that Russian program so much! I am so excited about it. When I think of my little girl having an opportunity like this! Why, I came from nothing! And here you might actually go to Yale and travel to Russia! At fourteen. It's as exciting as pageants, Scots."

9

※

Friday night, Father took Dane to the hotel where the contestants were staying. There were pageant chaperones, of course, so parents didn't have to stay. Saturday we drove up for the preliminaries, which lasted, as usual, several lifetimes. There were some very talented, photogenic, poised, and beautiful girls up against her.

"I see seven serious competitors," said my mother unhappily.

But we didn't tell Dane that. To Dane, we said, no contest.

We drove home around eleven that night, and Sunday we caravaned up to the pageant: our van first, with Mr. and Mrs. Gold and Lillie; then Grandma and Grandpa Barkley taking one neighbor family; Grandma and Grandpa McKane taking another; and then the bus. I wanted to be on the bus with the other kids and so did Lillie, but the bus was full because so many more kids came than we had expected. Bus, cars, and van honked the whole way.

"I had the most brilliant idea!" said my father. He usually drives leaning backward. Today he was hunched forward, so excited about where he was going.

"He really did," agreed Mother. The passenger seat in front swivels, and she swiveled around to face Mr. and Mrs. Gold and Lillie and me.

"For your Marsh Mid Princess Pageant talent, Scottie-Anne," said my father, "I'll follow you to Yale the first Saturday and film you on the campus! Film you saying your first Russian out loud and stuff. We'll have a big sign in the background that says EIGHTH GRADER GOES TO YALE! Whaddaya think? Is that a winner or not?"

"I think it's brilliant," said Mr. Gold.

"I would shoot you, Father! A *sign*? My father tagging around with his camera? I'll be this dumb little girl in pigtails and braces and freckles, while all these sophisticated older kids raise their eyebrows and laugh at me!"

"You don't have pigtails, braces, or freckles," protested my mother.

"But I'll feel like it," I said. "I'll feel lumpy and eighth gradey."

"She's right," said Lillie firmly. "You can't do that."

I looked at Lillie, glad because I had a best friend and an ally. Lillie was looking out the window, a funny, tight expression on her face.

"Why, Lillie Gold," said her mother in a shocked whisper. "Lillie Gold, you know perfectly well that's such a brilliant idea that Scottie-Anne could win with it. And you don't want her to win. You'd rather sabotage her. Your best friend! Lillie Gold, we haven't even arrived at the auditorium, and already I have just learned something about beauty pageants. They don't build character. They diminish it."

At the parking lot, the Marshfield High contingent poured out of the bus and cars. Four of the girls were cheerleaders and had brought their pompons. Our school colors are purple and white, and the varsity pompons are double: enormous, two-sided, papery whiffles, so the girls can go from white to purple and back. Shaking their pompons in each hand, the cheerleaders led the way.

"You aren't jealous of Dane?" Mr. Gold asked one of them.

The girl was amazed. "Heck, no. You wouldn't catch me subjecting myself to this. I mean, what if she loses?

In front of every friend she's got? It could be so humiliating. We're the audience. We get all the fun without any of the trouble." She bounded away, shaking pompons, shouting cheers. "Dane, Dane, she's our man, if she can't do it, nobody can!"

"It should be woman, not man," said Mrs. Gold.

"*Woman* doesn't rhyme with *can*," Lillie said.

Lillie and I tried to sneak into the dressing rooms to see Dane and tell her how huge the Marshfield contingent was, but the chaperone wouldn't let us in. So we just stood in the hall yelling "Dane!" until she heard and came to the door.

"How's it going?" I asked my sister.

Dane said, "I'm so nervous I'm going to throw up."

"You can't. I'll send for the school nurse to weigh you."

Dane giggled. Then she clutched me. "Scottie-Anne, I don't have a feel for this one. Everybody is so good. You should have seen the talents."

"I did see the talents, remember? And you were as good as anybody."

Dane said to Lillie, "I'm sure my sister is knifing me somehow, but I can't feel the blade. Has she gotten kinder? Or just craftier?"

"She wants you to win," said Lillie. "Her prestige is at stake. Anyway, my parents are here, and they have to be taught that beauty pageants are good things."

"That means if I lose, I have to do it gracefully,"

said Dane. "I hate being a graceful loser. I want to be a sore loser. I want to kick 'em if I lose."

I dared her to kick people. "I'll pay you," I promised.

"You'd probably get even better news coverage than if you won," Lillie pointed out.

"Young ladies," said the chaperone in a voice that left no room for discussion.

"Gotta go," said Dane.

"Break a leg!" I told her.

"Win!" Lillie yelled.

Back in the audience, we sat in a row of high school kids directly behind my mother and Lillie's mother, who were, predictably, arguing about the use and meaning of beauty pageants.

"It's a vicious, cynical world," said my mother. "A world in which innocent joggers are attacked by drug-crazed knifers. And in such a world, it's nice to have an event that has no purpose except beauty. Beverly, when you see your own child up there, illuminated by lights, and you're deafened by the sound of a huge audience clapping—for *your* daughter!—well, believe me, you'll be proud."

"I suppose," said Mrs. Gold carefully, "that I want to be proud of Lillie for other sorts of achievements. Things she wasn't born with, but worked for."

"Dane has worked," said my mother.

Mrs. Gold had no answer; by now she could quantify the work Dane put in. But no matter what, she still believed pageants weren't the same as musicianship and didn't merit the same applause and adulation.

"Show me the girl," said my mother, "who does not want to be Cinderella. Show me the girl who says, *No, I don't want the loveliest gown on earth, I don't want to dance with the prince!* Show me a girl who wants to be plain and ordinary and dull!"

"I suppose there isn't such a girl," admitted Mrs. Gold.

"This is the dream," said my mother, pointing to the scarlet velvet stage curtains and the gold-trimmed podium. "This is where it comes true."

"Whose dream?" said Mrs. Gold. "Yours or Dane's?"

"Both of ours, of course."

"But when Dane was little, you taught her to toddle down a runway in her crinoline and parasol."

"It was my dream then, of course. But Dane loved it! She became poised and relaxed; she couldn't wait to dress up and show off and get her crowns and roses and be photographed! She loved her videos. At home we'd watch them night after night."

"And how about Scottie-Anne?" asked Mrs. Gold. "How did she feel?"

We were spared answers. The pageant began.

We had the most supporters of anybody, or at least the noisiest. We screamed, cheered, bellowed, and applauded for Dane. A face squeezed between chairs, its chin fitting neatly between Lillie's elbow and my arm. "Nicholas!" I cried.

"Hi, Scots," he said. "Exciting, isn't it? I mean, I

think she's the best, better than anybody, don't you?" Nicholas turned out to have a great skill: He could put two fingers in his mouth and whistle loud enough to be heard in Oklahoma. The emcee even said, "Dane, is that your boyfriend out there?"

Dane, smiling into the lights that blinded her, with absolutely no idea who could be whistling, said, "I think he might be."

Nicholas squiggled in his seat like a little kid.

Lillie poked him hard. "Nicky has a cru-ush," she sang.

"You can have me, Nicholas," I offered.

"Or me," said Lillie.

Shannon jammed into the pack. I had probably never been so close to Shannon. "Nicky wants me," she said.

Nicholas kept his eyes on Dane.

Each contestant came out in an evening gown with her escort.

Bathing suits, known as "sportswear," had been Saturday and would not be repeated on Sunday even for the semifinalists, because "sportswear" is what has given beauty pageants a bad name. The press (if any; in New England, the press is notorious for not bothering; they give full-page interviews to high school football stars, but not so much as a caption under a photo for a beauty queen) were here today. It was best to give them as little ammunition as possible. Otherwise they would not write about the pageant, but about the cruelty of

Little League and the degrading nature of pageants. Little League always comes into it; whenever psychiatrists for adolescents discuss the dangers of pushy parents, they mention Little League and beauty pageants.

Dane was, of course, one of the eight semifinalists.

Micharde-Miquelle were there, having designed the gowns for three of those eight. They sat next to none of the families, but cruised the back of the auditorium nervously. Each gown was markedly different, but the Micharde-Miquelle trademarks were there: sequins, slits, and asymmetrical shoulders and necklines.

It was one of the few gowns Dane had that I disliked and disapproved of. The fabric was a glittery metallic weave which changed color depending on the lighting: As she turned, it gleamed peach, then rose, then pale yellow. Your eye caught the fabric, not Dane.

I began watching Micharde-Miquelle instead of the semifinalists. Their eyes were fixed on Number Eleven from Stonington. Stonington's gown was much more daring than most: crimson, more ruffled than slinky, yet far sexier, with no back and only a hint of front. They had used skin-colored gauze for the front, so your eyes searched for bosom details. By the time you realized Number Eleven was not nude, but swathed in nude-colored fabric, you had forgotten about Stonington herself, being far too concerned with whether her boobs were bare.

Mrs. Gold covered her eyes.

"Mom, we all have two of them," said Lillie. "Don't be so worried about it."

"If you appear in a gown like that . . ."

"You'd pay for that?" said Lillie. "Hah. You'll probably make me wear a white oxford shirt. Buttoned to the top."

Micharde-Miquelle blew it, I thought. They've gone too far. The winner is going to be Nineteen; that sweet, virginal wedding gown look is a lot more what the judges are looking for. In front of all her friends, Dane is going to be a runner-up at best.

Time to rejoice. War; and Dane was about to lose a big battle. In public. Time to sing in my cruelest whine, *Nannynanny boo boo. Nyah, nyah-nyah-nyah, nyah. Dane is a lo-ser.*

I knew that she knew. Dane's smile was strained. The hands which glided so gracefully cramped into frightened fists.

Dane would lose the USA-Connecticut T.E.N.E. and the scholarship.

I would win Yale and Marsh Mid Princess.

What would it be like having Dane in the backseat? Me with the crown and the cameras? Dane having to find contentment with her personality?

"What's her talent?" whispered Nicholas.

"Tap dancing," I said. I did not add that four of those eight semifinalists were also tap dancers, and that Dane was not the best.

The interviews came. Dane was first. She was visibly frightened. It had been years since I'd seen a crack in her poise. Mrs. Gold whispered, "I'm so nervous."

My mother nodded, knotting her purse straps around her hands like a hangman's noose.

"Dane," said the emcee in his big, bold voice, as if calling the troops to war, "what will you do with your life to make a difference to mankind?"

"*I've* never been able to figure that out!" whispered Mr. Gold. "How is a sixteen-year-old supposed to?"

Dane beamed at the emcee and sent a sweet smile to the audience. "I want to work with the elderly," she said, which was certainly news to me. "I want to help older people, the fastest-growing segment of our society. I think I could bring joy to—" out of phrases, she settled on another smile and a repeat, "the elderly."

The emcee snuggled up to Dane. "I need a little joy myself, Dane," he said, caressing her bare shoulder. "Maybe you could help me . . . back in my hotel room afterward, huh?"

Mrs. Gold gasped.

That kind of remark is not unusual. Men who emcee pageants are older, and this is how they feel about women. You have to put up with it.

My father went rigid with rage. Nicholas sucked in his breath and tightened his fists. My mother looked down.

But my sister, onstage, looked the emcee straight in the eye. She removed his hand. She took his mike, held it like a weapon, and said into the silence of a room filled with two thousand people, "The winner of the Teens Excel in National Events Scholarship Pageant will not be a hooker. Find one of them to help you."

112

10

The audience went wild.

"Give him a black eye, Dane!" yelled Mr. Gold.

"Atta girl!" yelled Nicholas.

High school kids stomped their feet. A row of people who weren't even from Marshfield gave her a standing ovation.

Dane, with the poise acquired in dozens of pageants, waved, inclined her head to the judges, allowed the emcee to have his microphone back, and gracefully, slowly, returned to the line of semifinalists.

My father leaned back.

"Did you get it?" whispered Mother, meaning the camera.

" 'Course I did. History in this film. I am so proud of her!"

"She'll lose now."

"But she went out in style," said Father. "I don't know how many times I've wanted to slug these emcees. But they've never said anything to my daughter before. Dane slugged him herself."

Of course, emcees aren't short on poise, either. This guy had done a million pageants, plenty of television work, probably dog shows and truck events in coliseums. So he hardly skipped a beat. "I owe Miss McKane, the contestants, the judges, and, of course, the families a sincere apology," he said immediately, looking sorrowful. "Beauty pageants deserve more than I just gave you. I thought it was funny, and, of course, it was not. I want to thank Miss McKane for her immediate and correct response." He paused for a moment to pay homage to his apology and then lifted his chin bravely with a the-show-must-go-on expression. "And now, with the shining attitude our times merit, ladies and gentlemen, judges, friends, families . . . number nineteen! From Roxbury! Miss! KellyAnn! Marie! O'Keefe!"

KellyAnn Marie O'Keefe's followers were few. A pitiful little round of applause escorted her forward. Belatedly, everybody else pitched in, until applause surged like a tidal wave.

We were close enough to see Dane well. There was a new expression on my sister's face. Peaceful. She knew she had lost; she no longer need worry or hope. She'd sleep well tonight, though we'd be five thousand dollars poorer.

But what else is new?

She even looked for us, which you never do onstage; it's so amateur to search the audience for your family. Father gave her the high sign, curled first finger and thumb; Mother blew a kiss; the Golds waved; I pantomimed a hug.

She gave us her real smile: the sad one, lips closed and curved like secrets.

The judges, of course, conferred and conferred and conferred and conferred.

"Does it always drag on like this?" said Mr. Gold.

My father said, "I would laugh if I were capable of it. Yes, always."

Onstage the girls performed their cowgirl routine.

Nicholas loved it. He sat on the edge of his seat, soaking it up. Dane was one of seven girls who kept coming out from behind the wooden cow silhouettes and doing a tap dance routine while holding on to the same jump rope. It was cute, which was good, since they did it so many times.

Mr. Gold said, "They have to pick Dane as the winner. After that answer? I mean, they've got to."

"You can't predict judges," said Mother.

"She'll lose," said Father. "You have to remember, pageants have percentages. It's done by calculator, actually. Say they give twenty percent to the talent. Tap dancing. Okay, she wasn't the best. She didn't get a ten. Probably got a seven-five. Interview is probably only ten percent, I don't actually know, but even if she got a ten, it's not going to cancel talent."

The cowgirl dance ended.

We applauded.

The judges conferred.

"But that's not fair," said Mrs. Gold. "For that answer she should win a hundred times over."

"But that wouldn't be fair," said my mother. "It's not a contest of Can You Put The Emcee In His Place."

The ROTC band from the university played a selection of tunes unfortunately written by one of them. Tuneless and noisy. "I would actually rather see the bathing suit contest than listen to another measure of that," said Mrs. Gold.

Everybody giggled insanely.

"And the judges are ready!" shouted the emcee.

Drumrolls began shivering from the back of the band. First on the metal rim of the snares, then on the stretched skin of the drums. Our hearts drummed along, picking up speed and volume.

The eight semifinalists, out of cowgirl and back into evening gown, moved slowly to center front.

Mrs. Gold said, "I just cannot believe Dane won't be the winner. We want Dane to represent Connecticut in the national contest! And the audience wants it! Surely the judges will take that standing ovation into consideration."

"Judges don't obey audiences." My mother was not on the edge of her seat. She was leaning back. Tired. Faded.

"And the third runner-up!" screamed the emcee.

It was a girl from Norwalk. Norwalk screamed and hugged herself.

"Mother, are you all right?" I whispered.

"I've never been better. It's all worth it. I never thought Dane would throw in the crown in order to set an attitude straight."

"And the second runner-up!" screamed the emcee.

A girl from Bridgeport. Bridgeport and Norwalk embraced.

My father whispered, just for us, "On the other hand, being strictly truthful, I wasn't happy with her situation to begin with."

"Ssssh," said Mother.

"You're right," I said to Father. "I think we need to change dressmakers."

"And the first runner-up!" screamed the emcee.

It was the girl from Watertown.

"That's my gut feeling, too," said Father. "That dress is a loser."

Norwalk, Bridgeport, and Watertown hopped in circles, hugging and waving to their cheering friends.

Dane stood quietly.

Stood *queenly.*

For the first time, despite all previous titles—princess, queen, miss—she ruled. She was right, she knew it, and that made her queen.

Mrs. Gold's fingers were interwoven like bootlaces. She was wetting her lips and tapping her foot nervously. Lillie was biting her nails. Nicholas was whispering, "She's gotta win, it's *gotta* be Dane!"

"And the winner!" cried the emcee.

He waved his envelope.

"Is!"

He looked back down at the words.

"Miss—"

The audience moaned.

"—USA . . . Connecticut! . . . Teens Excel in National Events!—"

"This is as bad as the Olympics," whispered Mr. Gold.

"Number nineteen, from Roxbury, Miss KellyAnn Marie O'Keefe!"

What I would like to know is how the news finds out that there is news going on.

Half an hour later, the lobby of the Sheraton was filled with media. The Hartford and New Haven television stations had cameramen there. There were also three newspapers, a stringer from *People* magazine, and a wire service, which meant every newspaper in the nation could pick up Dane's answer.

Nobody paid the slightest attention to Miss Kelly-Ann Marie O'Keefe, who had won.

"Miss McKane!" shouted a beefy woman, while her skinny runt of a cameraman knelt, jumped, and circled, taking photographs. "How do you feel about beauty pageants now? Do you despise them? You've been degraded publicly!"

"I am very proud of all the pageants of which I have been a part," said Dane softly, so they would hush to hear her. "And I was proud to be in this one. This is a scholarship event. Miss O'Keefe will be going on to the University of Bridgeport to study microbiology, and I think we've done a wonderful job raising funds to help her."

"Is she serious?" said Mr. Gold.

"Hard to tell," said my father. He was laughing now. He stopped when a camera began filming him.

"Mr. McKane, as the father of this young woman subjected to such a smear, how do you feel about beauty pageants? Do you think it was wrong to allow your minor daughter to become involved?"

"I'm very proud of my daughter," said Father. That was all they could get out of him. As for Mother, they didn't know who she was: She looked like a hotel porter, loaded down with bags, shoes, makeup cases, and mending kits.

Nobody asked me anything. Nobody held microphone, camera, or notebook to my face. I had never so completely been in the backseat.

Russia, smusha, who cared?

Dane had won, she always won. She'd even won the Golds, who on the ride home skipped seatbelts in order to lean forward and stick their heads right into the conversation with Dane, Mother, and Father.

I, Scottie-Anne McKane, with the double name, had nothing else to offer.

From my swivel seat in the back I caught my reflection in Dane's special mirrored alcove. A plain person stared back at me. Eyes swollen with unshed tears. Cheeks too thin, chin too large. Lips too straight, hair too dull. I hate you! I said to my reflection. You'll never be Miss Teenage America. You'll never be anything. Not even a Marsh Mid runner-up.

You're just a backstage, backseat nobody.

11

That week, however, a volcano erupted, a government toppled, a senator was accused of weird sexual practices, and inflation increased.

Although Dane stood poised on the edge of "going somewhere" (which is the whole point of pageants for many girls), she didn't. Nobody asked her to be on their television talk show. Nobody telephoned for more information or photographs. She appeared in two papers, toward the back, and not at all on television. They had other things to cover.

Dane could not believe it. She set the VCR to tape news on other channels, other hours. But no matter how often she watched, she did not appear.

How glad I was. I felt like standing on the back of the couch, taunt-dancing, *Nannynanny boo boo, they didn't like you.*

However, though Dane might not have won the world, she had won Marshfield. Teachers, parents of her friends, neighbors from our old neighborhood—they called. They were proud.

Marsh Mid Princess rehearsals became intensive. Dane took them seriously.

All week I felt like slime. My nasty thoughts sloshed around like jellyfish.

At Friday's assembly Mr. Shippee shushed us all and said, "Very, very, very important announcement, folks."

We rolled our eyes.

"We've had a singular honor, and I'm very proud of one of your fellow students."

We looked around. Whatever it was, even the student didn't know.

"Scottie-Anne McKane," said Mr. Shippee, "I am delighted to tell you that you are the only eighth grader in the state of Connecticut accepted into Yale University's Russian program."

I had done it. I couldn't believe it. Step one. Battle A.

I was building.

The kids of Middle School of Marshfield, Connecticut, were clapping for me, at last.

At lunch that day, Nicholas said, "Scots, this is so great! Congratulations."

Shannon said, "Why anybody would want to waste Saturday going to yet more school is beyond me."

"You'll be with geeks all bent over their books, bifocals at age sixteen, Scottie-Anne," said Eric. "It's not too late to get out of it."

"I could have gotten in," Lillie said, "but I am much too busy with my piano concerts and the Princess Pageant." I didn't answer her, but I wasn't too pleased with her comment.

Tasha said, "Scottie-Anne couldn't have won the Princess Pageant, anyway, so it's just as well she—"

"Shut up, Tasha, you slime bucket," said Nicholas. "People are different."

"That's right, Nicky." Shannon laughed, flouncing hips and hair. "Some of us are beautiful instead of intelligent."

I hate dumping on my mother, especially on a Friday. But I had to talk, and there was no Lillie now; Lillie was off with Dane and Mrs. Gold looking for a gown for the Princess Pageant! Mrs. Gold was not in favor of the Princess Pageant, but after seeing Dane tell off the emcee she said she'd fork over the money for a gown for Lillie. I didn't get asked to go shopping with them. Best friend or no, this was just Dane and Lillie.

"Mother, it was awful."

"It sounds awful. They're just jealous, Scots. Think of the honor! Only you, in the entire state of Connecticut, got into this program from eighth grade! I am so proud."

"Shannon says probably no other eighth grader was weird enough to apply."

"Let's make Shannon eat dirty sweat socks." My mother hugged me and leaned back, the way mothers do, for a longer, fuller look. "Oh, Scottie-Anne, I named you for your grandparents because they tried so hard. They've worked and worked to get somewhere, and when I couldn't finish high school, they wept and hated themselves. And look at you! Eighth grade and in Yale University! The world's finest college. My brilliant, thoughtful, intelligent, articulate daughter!"

"Mo-ther. Nobody else thinks that."

She was out of breath, as if we'd gone jogging. Her eyes glistened like Christmas lights. "Dane will have ribbons. But you, Scottie-Anne! You're going to have a stage, too. *It'll be the world.*"

The world, however, took very little notice of Scottie-Anne McKane.

My Saturdays at Yale began, but Father forgot about following me around with the camera. My parents didn't have to drive, after all; a Yale bus picked me up. At least I didn't sit alone; it was a small bus, with exactly enough seats, so though I didn't make friends, I had seatmates.

We studied Cyrillic letters. Learned about mountain ranges and mineral resources. Read a history of Russia prior to Peter the Great. Read short stories: Pushkin, Gogol, Chekhov.

I didn't talk much at Yale. The other kids were so much older. They, it was extremely clear, had not fibbed on their applications when they claimed lifelong interest in Russia.

I didn't talk at all in Marshfield.

Nobody asked me if the Volga River emptied into the Caspian Sea. Nobody cared how many kopecks in a ruble. Nobody was impressed that I was learning to decipher the headlines of *Pravda*. Gorbachev and what was happening in Lithuania meant nothing to my classmates.

I had guessed right all along.

Russia, smusha. If you want applause, win a basketball game or a beauty pageant. But don't win the privilege of going to classes on Saturday. Nobody cares. Nobody, even Lillie, ever asked me what I did each Saturday at Yale.

The Marsh Mid Princess Pageant was scheduled for January. The theory was it would break up the winter doldrums. The only one with doldrums was me. Mrs. Gold bought Lillie a gown, far too old for her, in my opinion, but the moment Lillie put it on, she looked old enough for it. She looked eighteen. She looked stunning.

I tried on Dane's old gowns. But the fifteen-pound difference in our weights, and the three inches in our heights, was too much. Nothing hung right, if it zipped at all.

Mother took me to several shops, but I wasn't shaped for sexy gowns: I was flat in the curvy parts and curvy in the flat parts. Colors weren't right, styles weren't right. We couldn't find anything to buy.

Wonderful eighth grade became this thing I stumbled through.

I felt so listless. I kept hoping I had mononucleosis, because then I'd have to go to the hospital. You can't rehearse for a pageant if you're on bed rest.

But the school nurse said it was just the winter blahs.

Practices for Marsh Mid went on and on and on and on.

The routine we were doing as a group was nothing like what I had expected. It seemed that Mrs. Craven was a sign language interpreter, and she had us learn three verses of "America the Beautiful" in sign language. Sung sign language sways like dance, and you use your whole arm as well as your hand and fingers. It's beautiful, and each gesture is surprisingly descriptive and easy to learn.

Shannon's community service was wonderful. She and her married sister prepared and delivered supper every night to a neighbor who was home dying of cancer. At first Shannon just did it to fulfill the requirement, but she really got into it, writing research papers for science and giving an oral presentation for English class speech.

Shannon. Who would have thought it? People began saying, "Shannon is really growing up; this pageant is so good for her."

Mrs. Gold is on the board of a hospice, where terribly sick people sometimes go instead of a hospital to die. Lillie went up twice a week to play the piano for patients. Anybody who was able got wheeled in, by bed or chair, and Lillie would play. She played everything from Christmas carols to ragtime. She learned sweet old country hymns for a sad and lonely old Baptist lady, and Brahms for a former college professor. Lillie became profound, and always had a topic, like death or beauty.

The other girls in Marsh Mid Princess expanded. I got smaller. Every morning when I dressed, it seemed to me there was less of me. Less personality, less heart, less interest.

Every time I thought about the pageant, I hunched in despair. I had no talent. No community service. No beauty. Even my grades were vanishing, getting smaller and smaller and smaller. I felt like Alice in Wonderland. I'd shrink too small for a dollhouse, no larger than the dot over an *i*.

One Saturday the Russian class went into New York City. We were going to the United Nations, where we would have the golden opportunity of meeting the delegate from the USSR. Everybody but me was so excited they could think of nothing else. We went in the same Yale pickup buses we took to class.

"Scottie-Anne," said the instructor in our bus, "I just have to tell you how interested I was in your sister's story." Dr. McGoldrick's an Irish-American former Catholic priest with a specialty in Soviet Jewry. You run into that kind of thing at Yale.

I could not believe it. Even Dr. McGoldrick knew about Dane. I had thought my beauty queen sister was at least not a part of this.

Mac, the boy who always sits across the aisle from me, said, "I saw her picture in the New Haven *Register* when she talked back to the emcee. She is gorgeous, Scottie-Anne. Does she look like that in real life?"

I tried not to hear him. Tried to be all by myself.

Catherine, two seats in front of Mac, got on her knees and turned around to talk to both of us. "I cut out her picture," she said. "I pasted it on the refrigerator to inspire myself to lose weight."

Jordy, Catherine's seatmate, got on his knees, too. "Can I have an introduction to your sister, Scottie-Anne? I want to take her to our school's winter dance and impress the socks off everybody else."

I thought: I'm going to cry. I'm going to be a stupid little eighth grader with a runny nose. "No, you can't have an introduction to my sister. What's the matter with me?" I tried to smile and be casual. "No, don't answer that," I said. "The list is too long."

128

"Scottie-Anne, my dear," said Dr. McGoldrick, remembering his priesthood a little late in the discussion, "at least you are brilliant."

I took off points for that "at least." With any luck he would end up in beauty pageant hell. "How would you know?" I said. "I lied on my application form."

"You did?" exclaimed Mac, fascinated. "Tell."

I quoted my lies. I explained how they were adapted from Dane's beauty-queen-interview fibs. The kids laughed so hard the bus driver said to quit or we'd tip over.

Dr. McGoldrick said, "I hereby accept your application, anyway, Scottie-Anne. So you don't know anything about Russia, after all?"

"I know what you've taught me."

"Hey, then you know one thousand percent more than the average American citizen," said Dr. McGoldrick.

Mac said, "Where do we have lunch? I'm already hungry."

"Make Scottie-Anne eat," said Lynn, from the back of the bus. Lynn is a senior, already accepted at Yale as a college student, planning to be a doctor. Lynn is as tiring as Dane. A winner all the way. She said, "You're too thin, Scottie-Anne. Would you like me to give you a lecture on nutrition?"

"No, she wouldn't," yelled Mac and Catherine in unison.

I have friends! I thought. I didn't even know it.

The skyline of New York City had never looked so

beautiful. Every reaching skyscraper looked like the hand of friendship. We toured the U.N., which I had already done on three previous field trips, but this one, of course, had a special touch. In a normally not-open-to-the-public conference room, we met with a Soviet delegation.

Dr. McGoldrick introduced each of us with a single sentence. About Lynn he said to them, "This young lady will be entering Yale in the fall and becoming a physician."

"A fine career," said the Russians politely.

About Mac he said, "This young man is a high school junior who has won a national science contest with his experiments on lasers."

The Russians almost bowed. They were courtly, as if their manners were from the time of the czars.

And about me, Dr. McGoldrick said—out loud— "This is Scottie-Anne McKane. Her sister is a beauty contest queen and has won many pageants."

The other kids stared at him, horrified.

I thought: I refuse to burst into tears in front of the Soviet delegation to the United Nations. There is such a thing as going too far.

The ambassador said, in excellent English, "We have just had the first beauty pageant in Moscow. It was very strange for us. You must be so proud of your sister, Miss McKane."

Stomping on his toes would probably not cement

130

Soviet-American relationships, so I said, "Very proud, sir."

A hint of smile tugged the corner of his mouth. "I think you lie, my dear."

"I think you're right," I said.

And the Soviet ambassador to the United Nations winked at me.

All the way home, Dr. McGoldrick kept repeating, "You became friends with the ambassador, Scottie-Anne. He talked to you for *ten whole minutes*! This is so exciting. I never dreamed anything like this would happen. I won't be able to eat dinner."

"Wait till you tell Dane!" said Mac.

"She's not going to tell Dane," said Catherine. "Don't tell Dane, Scottie-Anne. Keep it to yourself. It's yours, not hers."

"She has to tell," said Lynn. "It doesn't count if you don't tell."

We got into a Yale-type philosophical discussion of whether things count if nobody knows about them.

"Maybe you'll get an invitation to a dinner or a party at the embassy," said Dr. McGoldrick. "Can I be your escort? I know I'm fifty-six, but I could dye my hair."

"I'll be her escort!" yelled Mac.

"The whole class goes, or nobody," decreed Lynn.

"That's not fair," said Catherine. "Scottie-Anne made friends with him, the rest of us were just standing around."

"Life is not fair," said Lynn sternly.

That I had learned without the assistance of Yale University.

The bus arrived at the stop, and Father was there, in the van.

"Your parents are always there," marveled Mac. "My parents never remember. I have to telephone them, and half the time they aren't home, and I never know if they've already left to get me or gone somewhere else."

"See you next Saturday, Scottie-Anne!" yelled Catherine. "If you get any gold-trimmed Soviet invitations in the mail, you have to telephone us!"

"Eat a lot of supper!" said Lynn. "You're losing weight."

"Bye," shouted Mac.

I got out of the bus. Climbed into the van. Father gave me a kiss. "How was it?" he asked. "I haven't toured the U.N. since I was a kid."

"About the same, probably."

"Your mother used to want to be a U.N. tour guide."

"Why didn't she?"

"We got married too young."

I saw her suddenly: my mother, Grace, age seventeen, no high school diploma, no dreams come true. I saw her at work, amid noise and machines and deadly routine . . . saw Grace dressing her two-year-old Dane in ruffles and lace, putting her on a runway, holding

132

that gold trophy, caressing that satin sash, saving money for that video camera.

"Got one heck of a video for you to see after supper, Scots." He did a little waist-up dance of pleasure as he took the corner.

Mac was right. My parents were always there. Because they had no lives of their own! Because their only trophies in life were their daughters. Their lives revolved around chauffeuring and purchasing, scheduling and chaperoning, feeding and photographing.

I thought: No. I'm lucky. My parents are always there because they love us.

12

＊

"You never notice anything, Scottie-Anne," said my father. "If they ever need a witness to a bank robbery or identification of a passing car, you won't be any help."

"What do you mean by that?" I said indignantly. "I am a very observant person."

"Right," said Father, laughing. He turned off the living room light and started the video.

It was me.

Me at Yale. Dwarfed by creepy stone Yale buildings.

134

Shivering in the wind, lurching over snowbanks, slipping through iron gates. In front of a wall map of Russia, using a pointer to show the changing political face of Eastern Europe. Writing on a blackboard in Cyrillic letters.

Me in my best skirt and sweater for opening day; me in my worst jeans and sweatshirt later on.

"Father, who taped it? You weren't there!"

"I called your Dr. McGoldrick, of course, and told him that I needed a video and why. He got hold of a class member to do the videos."

"Who?"

"First you have to admit you never notice anything."

"I never notice anything! Who did this to me?"

"Nobody did it to you. *For* you, Scottie-Anne. Lynn did."

"Lynn? *Lynn knows I'm going to be in a beauty pageant?"*

"Sure. The whole class does. They're rooting for you. Now that you've seen the video, they don't have to keep it a secret anymore."

The video lasted two minutes, the maximum Mrs. Craven allowed anybody.

"Your Russian class is coming to the pageant, of course," said my mother eagerly, turning on the lights. "I've telephoned each student on your bus run. They'll have pizza here first. Then we'll caravan over to—"

"No!" I screamed. "You can't do this to me! Yale is mine! I'm quitting the pageant, I'm not being in it, I'd rather be dead!"

My father's big body looked little and hurt. His grin faded into fallen lips. "Scottie-Anne, I thought you'd be so pleased."

"Well, you're wrong! You trespassed on me! I had something of my own. I wasn't in the backseat. I hate you! I'm quitting the pageant! I'm quitting the Russian class! I'm quitting everything!"

"You cannot quit the pageant," said my sister fiercely. "Quitters are weak. Quitters are scum." She drove fast, not slowing down for potholes or corners. We slewed to the left.

"Quitters," I said, "are sensible."

Dane wrenched the wheel. She twisted on the seat, looked to her right, and parallel parked successfully— in traffic. "Mrs. Craven and I choreographed the group number for twenty-one girls, Scottie-Anne, and there are going to be twenty-one of you middle school creeps onstage if I have to sedate you and kick your limp body out on the runway. Got it?"

"I hate you."

"It's mutual. The dress I chose for you is at Viola's." She pointed out the window.

"Viola's! That fuddy-duddy, middle-aged, fat ladies' shop? Get lost."

"I traipsed over half the state and I found your dress in Viola's, so shut up and try it on and stop whining. You're just afraid of losing."

"I'm afraid of making a complete fool of myself in

front of people who matter," I shouted. Against my will I imagined my pageant gown: I would look like a southern belle on her plantation, my hair in banana curls, my waist thin as a wasp's, my skirt billowing with delicate lace and roses.

"All people matter!" said Dane. "Or are you already such a snob you think Yale people matter more than Marshfield people?"

The sidewalk was cracked and icy. Road salt crunched under my shoes. In Viola's, frumpy skirts and ugly suede suits hung around trying to look interesting. There were paisley scarves for grandmothers and wrap skirts for fat ladies. A store for middle-aged losers.

"Ah, Dane!" cooed the saleswoman. She was gaunt, dressed in many shades and textures of ivory, as if she were a display. "So this is your sister!" She beamed.

I stretched my lips, making a very minor effort at courtesy.

"You won't win a beauty pageant with that smile," said Dane irritably.

"I don't know," said the saleswoman. "I thought that smile had a sophisticated look. Intense. Very New York."

That was a nice thought. I found a mirror and stretched my lips again.

"She just wants to make a sale," Dane informed me. "Here's the gown. Put it on. I told Mother the price and she trusts my judgment."

It was not a fourteen-year-old girl's dress. It was a

woman's. Lillie's dress was old for her, but it made her eighteen and sexy. This would make me forty and pathetic. It was black and gray. It hung like a rag, twisting to the side as if cut wrong.

"It looks better on," said the saleswoman quickly.

I took it silently and went into the dressing room alone. Mother had insisted that we trust Dane's judgment. I trusted Dane, all right. She'd make me look like a candidate for lying in a casket. Slowly, I stripped off my clothes, folding them neatly, postponing the horror of the awful dress.

When I slid into it, the twist settled neatly; it was cut diagonally. Black satin and gleaming silver-gray curled in shimmering, slanting circles around my shoulders, waist, and hips, ending in a mermaid's tail by my left ankle. A slender ribbon of silver outlined the curls, and a metallic rosette glittered at my waist.

I came out.

Dane fastened a black ribbon high and tight around my throat, adjusting a rhinestone buckle in the center. With another black ribbon, she pulled half my hair up and away from my face, teasing the tendrils of the loose hair around my shoulders.

"There," she said. "That's you. You can't touch the wholesome all-American girl junk that I wear, and you can't go splashy and colorful like Lillie. You're understated and urban."

The saleswoman nodded. "Very New York."

138

I stared at myself in the three-way mirrors. Were they lying? Did I really look city sophisticate?

Or pathetic?

"Today we're going to practice answering pageant questions," said Dane. "Tasha, you're up first."

Tasha walked over the tops of the four cafeteria tables we used for a practice runway. Smiling at the ceiling, she surveyed the four corners of the room.

"Stop looking at the roof," said Dane impatiently. "The audience is lower. Meet their eyes."

Tasha met our eyes, giggled, put a hand over her mouth, covered her head with raised elbows, and said she wanted to start over.

"You can't start over," said Dane. "Once you start, you start. If you let the audience know you feel like a fool, it turns you into a fool."

"You got it," said Shannon comfortably. She was sitting cross-legged on the floor. "Tasha the fool."

"Whose side are you on?" said Tasha furiously.

Shannon smiled sweetly. "Mine." Shannon had decided chord organ was pretty limp and, since she was an excellent swimmer, was using a video of herself on the diving team for her talent. It was a golden opportunity to put a two-piece bathing suit into a pageant which did not have bathing suits.

This made Lillie furious. Lillie was now the only pageant entrant who was doing her talent live, and

Lillie now felt embarrassed and stupid about playing the piano at all.

"Shut up!" yelled Dane. "All right, here's your question, Tasha. If you could be any historical figure for one week, who would it be?"

"I don't like history," said Tasha.

"So what?" screamed Dane. "Answer the question!"

"I've never wanted to be some historical figure, though."

Shannon was now lying on her back on the cafeteria floor, laughing insanely into the fluorescent lights far above. "Eleanor Roosevelt," yelled Shannon for starters. "Marie Antoinette. Betsy Ross."

Tasha shook her head. "I'd rather be a rock star." Tasha had decided to lip sync with her favorite rock group instead of sing with her own voice. She bought a background video to bathe herself in vivid, pulsing lights. She wore very tight jeans and a shirt tied in a knot above her bare waist, her dance so sexy that middle schools nationwide probably had laws against it.

Dane had a tantrum. I was the only one who knew it. Everybody else thought my sister was overcome by a sudden need to tap dance. "It doesn't matter what you want, Tasha!" screamed Dane. "What matters is what the judges want. Shannon, you get up here."

Tasha jumped off, making faces and pouting. "I'm still gonna win, Shannon," she said when they passed.

Shannon laughed. "You? The best you can do is sing along with somebody who knows how."

Tasha's face turned angry. It made her features thin and cruel. Her nose, her lips narrowed; thin lines divided her forehead.

"Oooooh, this is fun," said one of the other girls. Singsong, she taunted, "Shannon ha-ates Tasha, Tasha ha-ates Shannon."

Shannon ran around to the far end, walked up the plastic milk crates we were using for stage steps, and came sexily forward, with much tossing of shoulder and revealing of thigh.

"Not very effective when you're wearing sweatpants," said Tasha viciously.

It made me sick inside.

Is there anything on earth worse than being laughed at?

The night of the pageant, when I emerged in a black and gray old lady's dress, would everybody explode with laughter—and then, a little late, pretend they were coughing?

"Shannon," said Dane in her emcee's voice, "you are entered in a very competitive pageant. Is it your opinion that there is too much competition in America?"

Shannon frowned. "I picked out a really good historical person to be, Dane. I don't care about competition."

"No two contestants get the same question," yelled Dane. "She answers hers and you answer yours!" Dane threw her notes to the floor, tantrumed another tap dance, and said to Mrs. Craven, "I hate this."

"I don't think you are a born teacher, dear," agreed

Mrs. Craven. "A teacher has to have a speck of patience to survive."

"But a student has to have a speck of brains. They aren't cooperating."

"It's the age," said Mrs. Craven comfortingly. "Middle school girls are low on cooperation. But I think we're getting a teensy bit tired. It's time for snacks, don't you think?"

Twenty-one middle school girls became very cooperative at the thought of food.

Mrs. Craven said to Dane, "Just a little tip, dear. No matter what age they are, you can solve a lot of problems with a chocolate chip cookie."

"You gain weight with a chocolate chip cookie," said Dane.

"But you feel good," said Mrs. Craven. "Here. Eat two."

"Did everybody have plenty of milk and cookies?" said Mrs. Craven. "Now. A quick update on everybody's community service. Tasha?"

"I'm helping my mother run my little brother's Cub Scout troop, and last week I was in charge of crafts. We're making Mother's and Father's Day gifts."

"Lovely. So good to work with children. I'm so proud. Shannon?"

"My sister and I are preparing meals every night for our neighbor with cancer. He especially likes my banana milk shakes. His doctor says his whole attitude and outlook on life have improved because of me."

"Oh, brilliant! So generous! Lillie?"

"I'm playing the piano each week at the hospice. I'm getting used to death and dying, and the hour I spend lifts the spirits of everybody there."

"My goodness, that's brave! I'm so impressed. Scottie-Anne?"

The linoleum was cold on my fanny, and the chocolate chip cookie left in my hand had crumbled.

I had forgotten community service.

"Scottie-Anne?" said Mrs. Craven again, looking up from her notebook.

Excuses. I had to think of an excuse. "I—I've been busy," I said.

The others stared.

"We're *all* busy, Scottie-Anne," said Shannon. "And *we* still fit in community service."

I wet my lips. Twenty middle school girls, including Lillie, regarded me with contempt. Lillie'd tell her mother . . . and somehow that hurt more than anything: I didn't want Mrs. Gold to know that I had never done anything good for anybody.

My heart hurt. It felt as if the valves were quitting the blood-pumping career. My whole chest was caving in.

Mankind was no better off because I was alive. I hadn't even picked up a piece of trash from the roadside.

I probably *am* the trash by the roadside, I thought.

I saw myself, the night of the pageant, in an old lady's dress, looking gray and pathetic while everyone else sparkled and sashayed. Silence instead of a list for community service. Everybody, even my Russian class, my parents, Mr. and Mrs. Gold, knowing that Scottie-Anne McKane was uncaring and a loser. Having to stand on the stage, hour after hour, while better girls won. A fake, desperate smile on my face. And afterward, the big lie all losers tell: "But I had the best time! It was worth it!"

13

"Mrs. Craven," I said, "I want to drop out of the pageant."

"Why, dear? Tell me what's wrong."

"Because I'm disqualified, anyway. I don't have a community service."

Mrs. Craven nodded, not so much agreeing with me as absorbing the problem. She's so heavy that her whole body nods along with her head. I had the weirdest desire to sit in her lap and be rocked. "Staying in the pageant will be your community service, then," she said gently. "If you quit now, it will spoil the group numbers, the printed program, and the spirit of friendship and joy we have nurtured in our pageant rehearsals."

Spirit of friendship and joy! Tasha and Shannon were each hoping the other would drop dead. Lillie was in a snit over the video-talent idea.

As for me, my spirit had turned out to be mean and selfish.

All along I had whispered to myself, *I'm not good enough to be in a pageant.*

But it turned out that I had never meant that.

What I really believed, deep down, was that I'm *too good* to bother.

Twenty girls chose to be nice, neighborly, and giving.

I chose to be selfish.

"Staying in the pageant isn't community service," I said to Mrs. Craven. I was trying so hard not to cry that I could feel all the muscles around my eyes. "It's punishment. It's torture."

Mrs. Craven looked into my eyes. "If you quit, Scottie-Anne, I shall be deeply disappointed in you."

The house was empty.

Mother and Father weren't home from work.

I didn't know where Dane was.

Deeply disappointed in me.

The words were stones being thrown at me. They

146

just kept coming, hitting me, making me feel worse and worse and worse.

And trapped.

I had to do it now.

There was no way out.

I started supper. The kitchen floor was sticky; knowing me, I'd probably spilled my orange juice. I mopped. There was a load of laundry to be folded, so I folded, and a wet load in the washer, so I threw it in the dryer. Then I decided I couldn't get through the night without brownies, so I opened a mix, made brownies, and shoved them in the oven.

In a way, I felt like my mother: Where, oh where, is lovely Friday? But I also had a wish foreign to her: Don't let Friday come! Because the day after Friday is Saturday—and a Russian class that knew all along about plain, dull Scottie-Anne trying to be in a beauty pageant.

"You're pitiful," said my father teasingly. I jumped a foot. I had thought the house was empty. "Burglars could be making off with the stereo and the silver, Scots, and you'd never know."

"We don't have any silver." I gave him a hug and got stabbed in the chest with a video camera. "Father, don't you ever put that down?"

"I'm taping you. You need community service."

With the foot-long knife I chopped leftover chicken and some onions. I love using that knife. I feel so

Chinese and professional. "I'm worthless, Father. I've never even helped an old lady across the street."

"If it's any comfort, I never have, either," said my father. "It's my impression that old ladies park their cars so they're on the right side of the street to start with."

I dumped a box of mixed vegetables and all the left-over rice in with the chicken and onions and opened a can of cream of celery soup. I took a ready-made pie shell, poured the mix in, inverted the upper shell, crimped the edges, and shoved it in the oven with the brownies. "Do you think we'll have chocolate-tasting chicken pie or chicken-tasting brownies?"

"I think we'll have a great supper," said my father, being relentlessly cheerful. "Charity begins at home, you know. This is you doing household chores without being told. That's a service." He had actually taped me crimping the edges of the pie shell.

"That's *family*," I shouted. "I have to have a *community* service, Father. And we're not using videos for service. We're using facts. The fact is, I've never done anything nice for anybody. I haven't thought of anybody but myself, ever."

"Dane, darling, what's wrong?" said Mother at dinner.

I planned my sentence. Or rather my paragraph. There was so much wrong, who even knew where to start?

148

But she was talking to Dane, who shrugged, smushing her chicken pot pie with her fork and leaving lines, as if to plant seeds in the fork furrows.

"Maybe actually eating would help you deal with your problem, Dane," I suggested. Not that Dane had any problems. Being beautiful keeps a good many of the world's problems away. "Some segments of mankind believe that caloric intake keeps the body alive. You could get wild and crazy and actually swallow food."

Dane smushed so hard her vegetables erupted like lava between the fork tines. "Mankind?" she repeated icily. "There's man, all right, but there's no *kind* in it. Man, woman, and sister—they're all vicious and worthless."

"Dane, darling, what do you mean?" said my mother. She can't bear it when we're in bad moods. It was going to be a long week for her.

"What's happened is, the Marsh Mid Princess Pageant is going so well, and Mrs. Craven has gotten such good publicity, and they've already raised hundreds of dollars in advertisements and still have ticket sales to go—well, the high school decided to have a beauty pageant, too. They haven't had one since 1962, and they decided this is the year to resurrect an old tradition."

"Darling, that's wonderful! Of course, you'll win! What fun!" My mother clasped her hands and bit her lips. I knew she was mentally sorting through Dane's gowns, deciding which she wanted friends and neighbors to see Dane in.

"It is not wonderful, and I won't win! The judges are going to be the president and vice president of each grade. What do they know about beauty pageants? It's going to be a personality contest. People like Jennie Fender are going to win, because all the boys adore her, and she's got two previous boyfriends holding office. People like Kathleen Marie Lonergan are going to win, because Kathleen Marie is always *doing* something for somebody."

"Is there a talent section?" said Mother anxiously.

"Yes, but it's not normal! Thanks to my worthless, rotten sister, they're going to allow videos for talent, too! That's so Jennie Fender can show herself getting her basketball team number retired! And so Kathleen Marie can show herself sitting at her sewing machine and making quilts for senile people, or whatever she does."

"At last," I said. "A chance to show off your spelling tests."

"Shut up, Scottie-Anne McKane, or I'll kill you!" screamed Dane. "I'm filled with hate right now, and if you want to stand in front of my fork, go right ahead."

"Girls," said Father.

"Now you have two daughters who are going to fail," I told him. "One who has never committed a service and one with no talent."

"You're dead, Scottie-Anne," said my sister. She got

up from the table and began circling the chairs. Since she had a knife as well as a fork, I decided to circle the other way.

My father said glumly, "Do you suppose other families act like this?"

"Other families probably get around to it sooner," said Dane. "I don't know why I've let Scottie-Anne's life drag on so long."

The place was knee-deep in pageants.

Everybody but me was happy.

I could not get over the fact that I had no community service to offer. That I was so selfish. Mrs. Craven's voice followed me around like a canary, singing, *Disappointed in you, disappointed in you.*

Naturally, there was nobody to tell except Mrs. Gold.

"Why am I telling you these things?" I said to Lillie's mother.

She tossed her head proudly. "Because you see in me a tremendous gift for understanding. Empathy, if you will, with youth."

"No," said Lillie, "it's because you're the only one home, Ma."

Mrs. Gold laughed. "What we need to analyze now, Scots—"

"Don't analyze. I hate analysis."

"I thrive on analysis. Why are you doing this pageant?" said Mrs. Gold. "You are whiplashing yourself, like some tortured medieval nun."

"A possibility," said Lillie thoughtfully. "Can you quick become a medieval nun, Scots? That's community service."

"I am doing this pageant, Mrs. Gold," I said fiercely, "because you forced me into it! You made me. It's all your fault."

Mrs. Gold stared. She got serious. "I forgot that. Scots, forgive me."

"I'll forgive you if you think of a community service. My father wants to show a video of me loading the dishwasher."

Lillie laughed so hard she folded up on the floor and nearly injured the dog. She said, "Oh, Scots, can't you just see it? There's you, in your old lady's gray and black gown, with a video of you folding napkins for the dining table. At least it would give everybody a good laugh. Being the comedian is a community service."

I had to remind myself that Lillie was my best friend.

I wanted to skip Yale, but even though I was now completely ruined there and humiliated forever, I didn't want to stay home Saturday while Mother and Dane tried to find a professional beauty pageant scheduled for the same weekend as the high school pageant, so she would have a perfect excuse for not being in, and losing, one so close to home. Never mind that *I* would lose the one close to home! It's Dane we have to save.

"I was taping the whole time," said Lynn complacently. "You are very unobservant, Scottie-Anne." She was crunching a large green Granny Smith apple. She also had a way of taking notes that made noise. How does a pencil make a racket?

"I am uninviting you to my pageant," I said to the class. "You are not welcome. I don't want you."

"Tough," said Mac. "We're coming. Solidarity."

"I don't want solidarity. I want to be unknown. Unrecognized."

"Spoken," said Dr. McGoldrick, "like a true diplomat. You know, Scottie-Anne, I feel that, for you, the world will be a stage. But you will be in the wings. You will engineer the drama. You will indeed be anonymous. But when great revolutions occur, when economies rise or fall, when elections and inventions change the earth, you will have been behind it."

There was a long pause in the classroom. We listened to Lynn's noisy pencil and apple.

Catherine piped up, "Hey. I plan to cause a few nations to rise and fall myself. Let's not give Scottie-Anne the entire globe. I want Japan."

"All I want is the patent on those inventions that are going to change the earth," said Mac. "Then Scottie-Anne and I will be incredibly rich, we'll retire from running the world, and live happily ever after."

There was a second long pause in the classroom.

"That's a proposal of marriage, Scottie-Anne," said Lynn, chewing apple. "Are you going to accept?"

"Yes."

The class cracked up laughing.

"Why?" asked Mac. He was grinning.

"It spares me the trouble of dating," I said.

Dr. McGoldrick decided this was enough silliness. He launched into the topic of Russia's war in Afghanistan and the legacy thereof.

After a while Mac sent me a note. He had to pass it through Lynn first, and of course she read it and appended her own message. Catherine intercepted, read it, and added to it. Mac, frowning, signaled to give it back. He read Lynn's and Catherine's additions and wrote below them.

At this point Dr. McGoldrick sighed, confiscated the whole missive, read it, and added *his* note.

It took half an hour to get to me.

The Afghan war? There are some things more boring than pageants, Scots . . . MAC.

Get a written confirmation of your marriage arrangement, Scots. There's room on the bottom of this sheet for your prenuptial agreement . . . LYNN.

Prenuptial Agreements are un-American and unromantic . . . CATHERINE.

I am giving a Russian-class winter party next Satur-
day. All-American romance guaranteed. All who
wish to come sign below . . .   MAC.

I will chaperone . . .   DR. M.

"Scottie-Anne's getting misty," observed one of the
other boys. "How mushy is this note, Mac?"

"It's a party invitation," said Mac. "To everybody.
Saturday."

I sat very quietly. Yes, yes, yes, yes, schedule a party
for next Saturday, save me, save my life, get me out of
town, who cares if I disappoint Mrs. Craven?

Lynn, whose mouth is as noisy as her pencil and
apple, said, "Reschedule, Mac. Her pageant is Saturday.
We are going to see the Marsh Mid Princess get
crowned."

I didn't go out to lunch with the rest. I hunched
behind the door and stayed alone in the room. Dr.
McGoldrick found me eventually. "What's the matter?"
he said gently. "We teased too much, didn't we? I'm
sorry."

I shrugged and turned away from him to mop up my
tears. I was on my last Kleenex. I had to stop crying,
anyway.

"It's not the class," I said finally.

"What is it, then?"

"It's the stupid pageant. I don't have a community

service." I told him all about the rules. About how a certain percent of judging would be in community service, and when mine was told to the judges, there wouldn't be anything to tell. I had failed. They would laugh at me and scorn me, and rightly so.

"Isn't this a community service?" said Dr. McGoldrick, gesturing at books, at Yale, at Russia. "You are going to be a leader of America one day, Scottie-Anne, I'm convinced of it. Acquiring knowledge and language is a service not only to Marshfield but to the world."

I just looked at him.

"Listen. I know the judges won't accept that," said Dr. McGoldrick. "I was running it by you to see how it sounded out loud."

"It sounded dumb."

He nodded. "But you said that Dane never really did her community service. She let your mother do the soup kitchen for her and wrote it down, anyway."

"That's all right for Dane. She doesn't mind. I mind! I want to have done something terrific and generous!"

He said, "Then you're almost there, Scottie-Anne. You know you *will* do good things. You know charity and neighborliness *will* be in your life."

"This is a fine time to turn back into a priest," I said irritably. "Who cares what lessons I've learned? The point is, a week from tonight I'm going to make a complete fool of myself in front of every person I know, including this class."

156

Some of the class, rot them, had tiptoed back from lunch.

They were listening through the door.

"You could run away from home," suggested Lynn's voice.

"Ask the Russian Embassy for sanctuary," said Catherine's voice. "They just developed a beauty pageant policy, and you could probably become the new Miss Moscow and star in yogurt commercials. Honestly, I just read that in the newspaper."

"I'll have my party on Saturday, after all," said Mac's voice. "Then you have a prior engagement you have to keep."

"I think I'll just commit a mass murder," I said, flinging open the door to attack, "and spend Saturday night in jail."

14

I spent the next week going without socks, mittens, and coat, hoping to get pneumonia and thus be in the hospital by zero hour.

No.

I remained healthy.

We now had a real beauty pageant–type runway, built by the woodworking teacher and some parents. I hoped to fall off and break an ankle. But it was wide, sturdy, and safe. I suppose I could have thrown myself off, but being a coward, I didn't.

Wednesday afternoon was our final group rehearsal.

We walked with our escorts for the first time.

Mrs. Craven had originally decided that each contestant should be escorted by her father, only to find that of twenty-one girls, seven had no father, stepfather, or even brother. So much for that.

Dane suggested that high school boys be drafted—ideally, the football team. High school football players turned out not to be excited about hanging around with thirteen- and fourteen-year-olds, even if they were future beauty queens.

We had to draft middle school boys. It was a problem. Some of the nicest hadn't started growing yet, and nobody wanted to walk down the runway with a boy who came up to her waist. And some who volunteered were too nauseating to associate with in public. Who would dress up like a princess in order to be seen with some of our more disgraceful and disgusting classmates?

Mrs. Craven, using enough diplomacy that I considered introducing her to the Russian ambassador—we needed Mrs. Cravens in this world—managed to find boys who were cute, didn't make anybody gag, and had a little height.

I drew Nicholas. I was so glad I nearly hugged him, which would have been fatal. At least my Russian class would see me with Nicholas, who was adorable. Maybe Mac would be jealous.

As if Mac, age seventeen, had any more real interest

in me than the football team. Mac just liked to kid around during class, and I was the easiest tease.

Maybe they won't come, I prayed. I wished I knew a prayer in Russian.

Nicholas seemed content with me, but Shannon and Tasha weren't. They flirted continually with him. He flirted back.

Thursday afternoon we were to practice walking in our heels and long hemlines. Some of us had never worn high heels, and just getting up the steps, standing on the risers, and pivoting on the runway was difficult.

Friday Mrs. Craven would do a walk-through with the band, the escorts, and the emcee (Mr. Shippee). There would be no traditional dress rehearsal because, said Mrs. Craven, it would detract from the excitement and tension necessary to a pageant.

I had none of the other necessities—such as beauty and community service—but I certainly qualified for tension.

So on Thursday we saw each other's gowns for the very first time.

I took my silver-gray and black gown to school, in a dark plastic dress bag.

We gathered in the cafeteria after school. Mrs. Craven taped heavy paper over the door windows so nobody could see in. She positioned herself in front of the doors to block anybody trying to enter. I felt jailed.

Tasha was the first to dress. Her gown was turquoise

blue, spangled with rhinestones, a silver ruffle cutting from one shoulder to the opposite ankle. Her heels, dyed to match, were high and spiky. She looked stunning. And her hair wasn't even fixed.

"The judges will be blind from Tasha's reflections," muttered Shannon, pulling silky stockings on her long, lovely legs. "Sequins," she said, "are tacky. Especially a hundred billion at a time." Shannon's stockings had a narrow, scarlet-embroidered flower and vine pattern up the side. Her gown was a shaft of crimson. When she walked, slits fell open to reveal her beautiful legs and delicate, daring stockings.

I could not make myself unzip my dress bag.

I would be a picture book illustration of Cinderella. My dress was literally a twisted, sooty-gray rag.

Dane has good taste, I told myself. I look fine in that gown. I look sophisticated and urban and New York.

I pretended to be Dane, who could lie awake all night thinking of nothing but victory. I pretended to be me, an elegant diplomat. Invited to all the secret rooms and private meetings of the world.

I tried to unzip the bag.

My fingers had become thick and spongy, like loaves of bread. My head ached and the buzz of excited voices attacked me like jackhammers in the street.

Lillie swirled among us.

Pianist that she was, Lillie had capitalized on concert black. Her gown was close-fitting, with a tremendous

161

amount of yardage in the skirt, so that when she sat at the piano, black satin cascaded around the bench, her waist feminine and delicate above it. The sleeves were long, with the prettiest wrist ruffles imaginable. The top was very low cut, outlined in long, soft black ruffles. With her dark hair and honey gold skin she, too, was a magazine cover.

Tasha and Shannon and the rest had sequins and glitter and prettiness. Lillie had elegance and grace and a difference.

I would just be odd.

As if I had worn a plaid skirt and an oxford shirt.

Bad enough when I got disqualified for no service.

How could I wear that old lady's dress in front of everybody?

"Mrs. Craven, I accidentally brought the wrong bag," I said to her. "I have to call my mother at work. She'll bring the right one. I have to go use the telephone."

"Fine, dear," said Mrs. Craven, letting me out.

I ran down the hall. The school was pretty much empty. I got to the pay phone row and called my mother at work. I was sobbing.

"Scottie-Anne!" said my mother. "Are you hurt? What happened? I'm coming. What's wrong?"

"I can't wear this dress, Mommy," I said. I had not called my mother Mommy in ten years.

There was a long silence on the phone.

I thought of my mother, at work: demands on every

side, exhaustion, and pressure. And now this annoying younger child whining about a dress. What did I think she was going to do about it? I had no other dress. Dane's dresses didn't fit. But I couldn't stop myself. Out it poured. "I know this one cost a lot, Mother. I know you trust Dane's judgment. But I don't want to be sophisticated and city. I want to be pretty and pageantish. Like everybody else. And ruffly. And lacy. With sequins."

The silence went on.

"Mother?" I said desperately. "Are you there?"

"I'm on my way," said my mother. "Meet me outside. The Blue Feather is the only possibility. They may have gotten prom gowns in."

The Blue Feather is a horrendously expensive boutique. The kind of place where you never actually meet anybody who has bought anything there, but everybody always knows what the new window display is.

"Mother, really? No, it's too much. What about your job, anyway? You can't leave work. Maybe we could alter one of Dane's."

"No, we couldn't. Will you stop being so thoughtful? I am tired of all your thoughtfulness, Scottie-Anne. Be selfish for once in your life."

I stood by the road, waiting. Mother was very quick. I could not believe how fast she got there. Her old wreck of a car roared up. It needed a new muffler.

163

Instead, we were getting a second expensive gown for a pageant we all knew I could not possibly win.

I could not stop crying.

"Scots, I want to do this," said Mother. "Stop crying. This'll be fun." She patted her purse. "Thank God for charge cards. Sky's the limit, Scots."

"But you thought Dane chose the right gown," I said.

"Yes, but trust gut feelings. If you couldn't even get the dress out of the bag, it's worthless. You have to feel beautiful, or you can't go onstage. Clothing counts."

We turned into the shopping center.

"I didn't even go back to tell Mrs. Craven what's happening," I said.

"I'll call her later. Don't be so worried, honey. It's only one rehearsal, you've been to the other fifty."

We didn't lock the car. Impossible to imagine anybody stealing it.

"I know exactly what I want, Mother," I told her.

"That's not good. You never find anything if you know exactly what you want."

"I want it ruffled and lacy and layered and sparkly and perfect."

My mother laughed. "Me, too. In fact, I wanted my life to be like that."

The Blue Feather had just changed windows. Prom gowns were in. "Show us everything," Mother told the clerk. "We want to be lacy and ruffled and sparkly and perfect."

164

"And layered," I said.

The clerk actually clapped her hands. "I have the dress," she said.

For a moment she stood in front of the gowns, blocking our view. Then she stepped back, introducing the gown with her hand.

And there was the dress.

Dark, deep green moire that changed color like the sea. The skirt cascaded in layers, each rimmed with velvet ribbon and a lace overlay. Tiny poufed sleeves and a diamond cut-out back.

I was in love with it. I was so excited I was out of breath. I had never seen such a dress. Not on my body.

"I've never seen such a price tag," said my mother.

"We don't have to get it," I said quickly. I wanted it so much I could hardly breathe at all.

"Of course, we have to get it," said my mother. "It's perfect. I don't know how I ever let you keep the other one."

15

It was a good year for trumpets. The high school band sounded like solid brass. Forty-five of us stood in the wings listening to the band warm up: twenty-one contestants, twenty-one escorts, Mr. Shippee, Mrs. Craven, and Dane.

Dane peeked through the stage curtains. "Full house," she reported. Dane was adjusting gowns here, changing makeup or repinning hair. To every girl she had something encouraging to say.

I had known that my sister, as our friendly local

beauty queen, would present the crown to the winner of Marsh Mid Princess. But it had not sunk in until we were both at Tangles, having our hair done. The perfumed scent of shampoo and conditioner filled the air, while humming blow-dryers made people raise their voices. They talked of Dane, her victories, titles, and future. Michael, who owns Tangles, spent two hours on Dane, while Noreen, who had just finished hairdressing school, spent twenty minutes on my hair and then asked Michael if it would do. Michael barely glanced my way. "Sure, that's good," he said. In Dane's hair Michael sprayed gold glitter. Since she was no longer entitled to wear a crown herself, being a last year's winner of everything, he fixed a garland of gold ribbons in her hair instead.

Dane wore the slinkiest gown she owned: a knit tube entirely covered with gold sequins, slit to the thigh. She and Mother had finally located an important-sounding pageant in New York state the weekend of the threatening high school pageant, which spared her that terror.

I admired Dane. She was stacking the deck in her favor, but how else do you stay alive in her game? I had a sense of Dane storming the fortress: Dane, equipped with gowns and mirrors and runways, fighting on, elbowing through. Get off the battlefield if you're going to lose. But never surrender.

Next to Dane, all but one of us were just little girls pretending to be beautiful women. Lillie was that one.

I could live with Lillie winning. The question was, could Mr. and Mrs. Gold?

"What were your parents saying that depressed you?" whispered Lillie.

I pretended I didn't know what she was talking about.

"When all our parents were at the stage door wishing us good luck before they sat down," Lillie pressed.

I shrugged.

"Come on. Tell me."

"It doesn't matter whether you win or lose, it's how you play the game," I repeated. "That's so stupid. It *does* matter whether you win or lose! And furthermore, how I played the game was, I skipped community service."

Mrs. Craven was circling also, giving out hugs and simple instructions. "Have fun!"

Fun, I thought. Right. "What about my community service?" I said.

"It's lovely, dear, and I'm so proud." Mrs. Craven moved on to Shannon and then Tasha.

Lillie giggled. "It's that video of you loading the dishwasher, Scots."

My hands became sweaty, cold lumps stuck to the ends of my arms. They hung awkwardly, as if I were carrying five-pound bags of sugar. Mrs. Craven had forgotten that I had none. She had mixed me up with somebody else. Or had my father actually brought a video of me folding laundry?

I have to die, I thought. Quickly.

We were away from all mirrors now. I ran the green fabric through my fingers to remember what I looked like. My green gown was protection. I matched. Once I was disqualified, I would go back to the lineup and blend in and disappear and live through it.

"I didn't sleep all night," proclaimed Shannon.

"I never sleep before a pageant," Dane admitted. "I lie there imagining myself the winner. I imagine every step, every move, every beat of music."

"Do you ever imagine yourself the loser?" asked Tasha.

Dane was appalled. "Never."

We fidgeted. Worried. Took deep breaths, but not too deep: Most of us had gowns so tight that deep breathing would have to wait.

"I love your dress," said Nicholas to me. "We've bagged it, Scots, I can already tell."

Mr. Shippee paced, reviewing notes, muttering, ". . . devoted to her hobby of . . . especially interested in . . . expectations are greatest for . . ."

"Your Russian class is here, Scots," whispered Dane. "Two of those boys are adorable."

"They think you are, too," I said dutifully.

"I know. They told me so. Good luck, Scots."

"Are you mad about my changing gowns?"

"No. You're absolutely right. This green one's better. It's perfect."

I studied her. "I never know when you're telling the truth, Dane."

"I never know, either. I use it so little."

We smothered laughter. Sometimes Dane and I are suddenly sisters, who understand, laugh at the same things, and even love each other. If only it happened more than twice a year! Mr. Shippee called Dane over to ask her something. Half-shadowed by backlights, Dane was so lovely, so golden, so fair and beautiful!

I had a gown, I had scholarship, personality, and probably someday I would commit a service.

But I did not have beauty. I would never have beauty.

Nicholas said, "Calm down, Scots. Look happy and sleek."

"Sleek?"

"That's how your sister always looks. Like my golden retriever after he goes to the vet for a shampoo."

"You must tell Dane that."

"Okay," said Nicholas, looking around for Dane.

"I'm kidding. Never tell Dane that."

"Why not?"

"Beauty queens hardly ever like being compared to dogs, Nicky."

The band finished its opening numbers. Mr. Shippee took the podium. We straightened our lines, our skirts, and our minds.

"Smile, dummy," muttered my sister. "Where are your teeth? What's the matter with you?"

I showed some teeth.

Nicholas said, "You're not supposed to look as if you want to bite, Scots."

I giggled hysterically. Death was coming. It would be an anonymous sort of death, until, of course, Monday, when at school everybody would let me know the gory details.

The line moved.

One by one, each girl with her escort emerged from backstage, between a tiny forest of donated potted palm trees, under a wooden trellis draped with silk roses, and onto the center of the stage.

Thank God for Nicholas.

I had lost control not only of my hands, but also of my eyes and brain. I could hardly pick up my feet, either. The voice of Mr. Shippee, so well known, sounded like opera underwater.

"This is so much fun," whispered Nicholas. "I love having an audience staring at me."

Luckily, I was blinded by spotlights and could not distinguish the audience. Whistles, stamping, and clapping were accompanied by flashbulbs as we were immortalized by loving parents, brothers, sisters, aunts, uncles, grandparents, and friends.

"Come on," whispered Nicholas. "What are you waiting for?"

"Huh?"

"It's our turn."

I had not heard a thing. But Nicholas was walking,

and I was attached to him, clinging like Velcro to his jacket sleeve, so I, too, went forward. Nicholas and I hit the first red-taped X on the runway and he turned me in a circle, as if we were dancers. This was unrehearsed, but Nicholas must have figured that, without him, I would just lie down on the runway and hope to be carried off.

I smiled like an insane person at the band, whose front row frowned back, as if realizing for the first time that insanity does rule on this earth: Beauty pageants are proof. I don't know how much grace and beauty I managed, but Nicholas filled in for me. Through the clapping came a yell, "Hey, Nicky, whose beauty contest is this?"

Nicholas was laughing. "I gotta become an actor, Scots. This is the life. They're all looking at me."

"Scottie-Anne McKane is in eighth grade," intoned Mr. Shippee. The microphone grabbed each word and threw it relentlessly into the public ear. "One of our best students, she was chosen for Yale University's special program in Russian language and culture and spends her Saturdays in New Haven, adding a sixth day of school to a very busy schedule."

Mac, Lynn, Catherine, and Dr. McGoldrick were yelling "We love you" in Russian. It sounded so funny, in the auditorium of Marshfield Middle School.

"Wave," ordered Nicholas. Like Dane, he could speak under his breath and never stop smiling.

We were at the end of the runway. My torture was

half over. And I could have my back to the audience for the rest of it. Perhaps they would be so busy admiring the diamond cutout they would ignore the fact that I had no service.

"Painful as it is to admit . . ." announced Mr. Shippee.

He was going to yell at me. In public. Over the microphone.

". . . last year our school had a drug problem. Scottie-Anne organized a monitor system to keep our school safe. She has supervised her twelve volunteers all year."

Monitoring. So hateful and thankless, I had made myself forget.

Last year, marijuana smoking in the bathrooms scared kids off. Parents refused to admit the problem. After all, who wants to admit twelve-, thirteen-, and four-teen-year-olds are using drugs? The teachers couldn't spend class time in the bathrooms, the janitors said it wasn't their responsibility, everybody was pretending it wasn't happening, anyway—so Mr. Shippee took the bathroom doors off.

This did stop drugs, but it also stopped going to the bathroom, which for most of us is a fairly regular activity. So I organized eighth grade monitors. I have to see they don't accept payoffs, get scared away, lose interest, or skip turns. There is nothing worse than turning your classmates in. Except, I guess, a school where nice people are afraid to use the bathroom.

"Scottie-Anne's dedication and perseverence," said

Mr. Shippee into the mike, "have been a major contribution in helping to keep our school drug free."

He was exaggerating. My turn came only once a week. He saw I had no community service listed, I thought, so he remembered one and turned it into something special. My eyes flooded. What a gift!

"Mr. Shippee's a jerk, isn't he?" Nicholas whispered. "People are still doing drugs. They've just quit using the bathrooms."

I suppose getting the doors back on was a form of diplomacy. Nicholas was right: I had accomplished little. But everybody was happier. Perhaps that is diplomacy: Make people feel better without changing much.

Oh, cynical Scottie-Anne! I thought . . . and then the real cynicism struck: The real diplomat is Mr. Shippee. Getting free credit and exposure for being brave enough to admit a drug problem and clever enough to conquer it.

We were off the runway. Only a few more steps to stage left, where we would position ourselves for the duration. My eyes went back into focus. I could actually see the other girls now: their dresses and expressions and hairstyles.

Shannon was glaring.

Tasha's eyes were wide and calculating.

Lillie looked amazed.

I, Scottie-Anne McKane, had just become competition.

"Scots, we've bagged it!" chortled Nicholas. "We're the princess."

I had a chance. I could win. My sister could crown *me.* My heart, moments before hardly strong enough to keep me in a coma, leapt into the future, pumping hope and plans.

Marsh Mid Princess, I thought giddily. Young Miss Connecticut. Miss Teenage America! Scottie-Anne McKane, beauty queen.

My hands turned back into hands. My feet were able to carry me up one riser. And my brain, functioning again, had a thought. (I would have preferred to stay nonfunctioning.)

I didn't care about drug-free bathrooms.

I didn't care about being generous and helpful to my community and my school.

All I cared about was looking good. My community service was no gift; it was just like mascara or hair spray. I put it on to look good.

"Don't cry," whispered Nicholas, alarmed. "The tough part is over."

The tough part had just begun.

Knowing myself.

16

Every talent except Lillie's was on videotape.

The gleaming stage grand piano—black as midnight—was rolled forward at Lillie's imperious signal. She played a medley she and her teacher had devised, slipping from ragtime to Chopin to Beatles and back in two minutes. It was wonderful! She was so lovely, her dark, romantic hair, narrow waist, black cloud of satin falling to the floor.

Lillie accepted her applause and swept past to take her place behind me. "How was I, Scots?" she murmured.

176

"Flawless. Beautiful. Magnificent."

"I thought so, too."

We laughed softly. I said, "Considered modesty as a virtue lately?"

"Modesty is not a virtue. How can you go onstage if you're modest?"

"Don't you love the stage?" whispered Nicholas.

"Yes," said Lillie. "It's me. Forever. I don't care if it's acting, pageants, or concerts. This stage is my spot in life."

Why anybody would want to torture herself more than once on this ghastly public platform under these ghastly exposing lights was more than I could comprehend.

Shannon's diving video was next, her tan hardly divided by the scrap of bathing suit. She was impressive.

My video was pathetic. Unfocused faces, distant, unidentifiable Yale buildings, and a narration by my father so filled with pride even Dane looked away, blushing. But Nicholas said, "Bagged, Scots. It is *us*. Who is that guy who keeps standing up and taking photographs of you?"

"My father."

"No, no, no, not your father. The young one."

It was Mac. I said rather giddily, "Friend of mine at Yale who proposes all the time."

"You lead the most exciting life," said Nicholas enviously.

Mr. Shippee was now showing a video of his own. It didn't seem to be about us. Some woman I'd never seen was holding up books. ". . . successful fund-raiser we've ever had!" shouted Mr. Shippee. "The new set of encyclopedias will be ordered tomorrow, and we have money left over for expansion of our computer library as well! Thank you so much, participants, parents, and friends!"

I had completely forgotten encyclopedias—the purpose of all this torture and effort. Up-to-date reference books. "Next time," I muttered to Nicholas, "remind me to earn the money myself and just donate a set to the school."

I had to say good-bye to Nicholas then. The escorts were marched off. The band played while we changed into our costumes for the "fitness routine and program event," which Dane had helped choreograph. It went pretty well, considering that I started backward and Shannon kicked me to turn me around.

We finished the routine, bowed, and the curtain closed for us to change back into evening gowns. It was pretty frantic, because we'd gotten sweaty, and our hair was out of place, and nobody could find her own hairbrush.

Once again onstage, the twenty-one of us stood in three neat, seven-girl rows. The judges had finished.

The four semifinalists were to be named.

In spite of all the orders I gave to my body, my hands turned into five-pound bags of sugar again, my

eyes went blind, my ears went deaf, and my feet solidi-
fied and became part of the stage floor.

"In no order, ladies and gentlemen," cried Mr.
Shippee, having a wonderful time, obviously as stage-
struck as Nicholas, "I have the privilege of naming the
four semifinalists of the Marshfield Middle School Princess Pageant!"

The audience applauded wildly.

"Tasha—"

You couldn't even hear her last name over the stomping
and screaming. Tasha, giggling, silly-acting, thrilled,
stood next to Mr. Shippee.

"Shannon—"

Shannon, calm, sure of herself, joined Tasha and gave
her a sweet, affectionate hug. A Dane hug. I knew that
kind of hug. One hundred percent fake.

"Lillie Gold!"

I applauded harder. Lillie reacted like a real person.
She flung back her head, laughed out loud, hugged
herself, and ran up to Shannon and Tasha. No fake hug
for Lillie. She put out her palms for a basketball court
slap. Shannon and Tasha were irked, but had no choice,
and slapped.

One more minute and it would be over.

One more minute of pretending, faking, acting, hiding, and I would be done.

I stood still, trying to breathe, trying to get past it
all, trying to have self-control.

"Scottie-Anne McKane!" shouted Mr. Shippee.

Me.

Me? I actually mouthed to Mr. Shippee, *Me?* and he actually smiled. Nodded. *You.*

And that was when the beauty pageant began.

There was no more mention of scholarship or service.

One by one, Tasha, Shannon, Lillie, and I displayed ourselves.

I had less to display. There is no other way to put it. I'm just me.

My jaw ached from smiling, like a year at the dentist's. I lost my smile. Just had lip twitches. There was no Nicholas to lean on. How narrow the runway seemed now. How tippy. Spotlights tried to distract me and pitch me off—break my ankle—now that it was too late to do any good.

Real time, clock time, stopped.

Infinity began.

The judges conferred.

The girls rustled.

The audience murmured.

My heart cried, *Let me win, let me win.*

The band played two more pieces.

The judges handed an envelope to Mr. Shippee.

Dane, gold and shimmering, stepped forward, holding in her fair hands a filigree crown. Beside her, on a tiny white table, lay bouquets of red roses. For the losers.

Mr. Shippee asked the four semifinalists to step forward.

Tasha was actually moaning.

If I'm moaning out loud, God, I prayed, *kill me.*

Mr. Shippee held the envelope up to the light.

The audience moaned, too.

Lillie stood regal as a queen.

Shannon stood sexy as a centerfold.

Tasha moaned.

I didn't know what I was doing. I couldn't even bear to think about it.

He opened the envelope.

He read the names to himself.

Then he said, "Ladies and gentlemen."

The man's a sadist, I thought.

"Students," said Mr. Shippee. "Friends. Relatives. Sponsors."

Why not add the President of the United States? The governor of Connecticut? Anything to string it out.

"The third runner-up!" shouted Mr. Shippee.

Audience hands were in the air, separated, ready to clap.

"Is Scottie-Anne McKane!"

The audience began stomping and whistling. I can't imagine why. Third runner-up is the loser! Dane pressed her pretty, fair cheek against mine and handed me my red roses. "You whipped seventeen out of twenty-one, kid," she whispered. "Not bad."

But we both knew better.

I had not won. I was a runner-up. Dane's definition of runner-up was: *Nothing*.

Mr. Shippee kissed me, which was disorienting. You don't normally run around kissing your school principal. I waved to the audience and tried not to cry. But, of course, they had lost interest in me. I was nothing. They wanted to find out—

"The second runner-up!" shouted Mr. Shippee, "Is! Lillie! Gold!"

Beautiful, talented Lillie had lost?

Lillie, too, smiled, waved, bowed. But when she joined me, her bouquet of roses dramatic against her black ruffles, her eyes were full of shocked tears. "I lost," she whispered numbly.

"We have to hug," I whispered back.

She hugged, forgetting roses. We crushed them between us. Her hug was fierce. We're still best friends, I thought. We each lost. Did that keep us friends? Would one a winner and one a loser have lost us friends?

"First runner-up!" shouted Mr. Shippee, beaming, "Is Tasha!"

Lillie whispered, "The worst part will be hugging Tasha. That'll take acting."

But poor Tasha did not even get her share of applause, because now the audience knew that Shannon was the winner, and it was Shannon who got the attention now.

Shannon who counted.

Shannon and only Shannon.

The rest of us were wallpaper.

How alike Dane and Shannon were.

In the end, nothing matters but conventional beauty.

You must have white teeth, lots of them.

Poise, out of all proportion to what you have actually accomplished on earth.

Shiny, thick hair, a lovely dress, a sexy walk, and long, slim legs.

Service and scholarship are so much fluff.

My mother gleamed. The shining happiness she had when Dane won. "I'm so proud," she cried, embracing me.

"But I *lost.*" I felt so doomed and useless, ugly and dull.

"Lost!" My mother laughed. "Dane won't enter anything she can't win. She has poise, but she doesn't have courage. You were so brave to enter. I was so proud. You were so beautiful."

My Russian class stormed forward, surrounding me with hugs and cameras. "You failed me, Scottie-Anne," said Mac. "I wanted you to make history."

"I will," I said. "I'll be the first third-runner-up from Connecticut to go to Moscow."

My father videotaped on and on. "Say something in Russian," he ordered us. We said something in Russian. My mother clapped her hands. "Only four more months, and you board a plane for Russia! I just can't stand it, I'm so proud."

Mr. and Mrs. Gold took a couple of pictures. "I was

convinced," said Mrs. Gold sadly, "that Lillie with her piano or Scottie-Anne with her Russian would be Marsh Mid Princess."

"Why, Mrs. Gold," said Dane, a wicked, triumphant grin crossing her face. "You are sad. You are grieving. You wanted your daughter to be Marsh Mid Princess. Admit it, Mrs. Gold!"

Mrs. Gold frowned slightly. "Well, it isn't so much that as that I just can't feel that Shannon was quite as qualified."

"Hah!" shrieked Dane. "You wanted Lillie to win! The janitor told me you came over this afternoon to polish the grand piano, so it would gleam while Lillie played."

"Well," said Mrs. Gold finally, "well. All right. Yes. I admit it. I wanted Lillie to win."

Dane smirked. "Conventional always wins. Shannon has conventional beauty contest looks. Lillie doesn't."

"I hate the moral of this story," said Mrs. Gold.

"I don't," said Dane. "I like winning." She admired herself, her gown, and her victory over the Golds. "Let me rephrase that. I *love* winning." Dane laughed, and left us, to circulate among the seventeen who had not placed. . . . "You were the best dancer in the group number, Janet." "You have to keep wearing your hair like that, Erin." "Whenever you smiled at the audience, Megan, I just felt such personality coming from you!" She didn't miss a single contestant. She had something terrific to say to each girl, and she managed to say it with the parents there, so they could share.

Mr. Gold said, "You realize, Lillie, that you were the only person in this whole show with the guts to risk making a mistake in front of people? Everybody else had a video that they could film over and over till it was perfect."

Lillie nodded. "I held that audience. They were mine. I loved that. But, Daddy, I wanted to win." She no longer looked regal and exotic. She looked fourteen and disappointed. "I wanted to go on! And be Miss Teenage America! And be a star, and famous, and beautiful."

Didn't we all.

"You are Miss Teenage America," said her father. "Every girl is Miss Teenage America to her parents."

"Big deal," said Lillie. "Parents don't have a choice. They have to think that. I want the world to think it, too."

But parents don't have to think that.

Two girls in the pageant—their parents didn't even come.

There was a boy in my grade whose parents had not come to a parent/teacher conference since kindergarten. Another who never had lunch until he got old enough to make his own sandwich at home, and even then there wasn't always food to make it out of: His parents didn't care enough about him to buy groceries. There was a girl when I was in sixth grade, her parents got a divorce, and far from fighting over custody, they each told the judge they didn't want her!

My mother glowed, telling everybody how she had come from nothing, and here was her daughter, placing in beauty pageants, speaking Russian, and going to Yale. I thought of her leaving work, coming for me, buying the second dress.

My father videotaped on and on, getting the outdated set of encyclopedias, for heaven's sake, on which he insisted I rest my hand while he filmed. I thought of him calling Dr. McGoldrick, getting a camcorder to Lynn, hugging his secret video to himself.

Mrs. Gold . . . who disapproved of the whole thing, coming over here and *polishing the piano*.

Mr. Shippee . . . reading through his notes, seeing that one girl hadn't listed a community service, putting one down himself, making a big deal over something that isn't big.

A reporter from the local weekly had difficulty getting the story right. I had to spell my name twice and explain to him why a third-runner-up actually came in fourth.

"Are you glad you were in the pageant, Miss Mc-Kane?" His pencil was poised, his eyes on his notebook, waiting for words.

"Yes," I said. "I'm glad. I loved every minute of it."

J
F
CO

Cooney, Caroline B.

Twenty pageants
later

$15.00   WITHDRAWN

	DATE		
JUN 24 '92	FEB 0 7 2002		
JUL 5 '91			
JUL 1 6 1991			
AUG 2 0 1991	AUG 2 3 2004		
	MAR 2 7		
DEC 1 4	SEP 2 2 2009		
JUN 2 5 1992	MAR 2 8 2016		
AUG 1 4 1992			
AUG 1 0 1993			
AUG 2 4 1993			
JAN 2 5 1994			
DEC 2 7 '01			

WITHDRAWN

5 - 91